THE
SUICIDE
BRIDGE

HANNAH KATHERINE KLUMB

The Suicide Bridge
Copyright © 2018 by Hannah Katherine Klumb
Waterton Publishing Company

ISBN 978-0-9905249-6-0

WATERTON
PUBLISHING COMPANY
watertonpublishing.com

For Steve, who motivated me to never give up. Thank you for staying by my side in this journey. Always.

PROLOGUE

I sn't it funny how the things we long to forget stay with us the longest? Or how much we revel in the adrenaline rush of a horror movie just to escape our own demons? Now, before you think I've gone insane, let me tell you how I know I'm not the psychopath, but unfortunately my dear friend, you might be one yourself. See, I've accepted reality. That harsh truth we gave the sobriquet to by calling it our life. Once you realize your true reality, you become the sanest person this planet has ever known. It is miserable.

Sometimes I question why I chose this dark path. Certainly not for society's approval, as it has made me into a recluse. Ironically, perhaps I did choose it because of society, though only as a means of proving them wrong. All those glossy photoshopped magazines are actually instruction manuals for how to clone yourself into being one of the world's robots. The ideal body type, hair, attitude, whatever it may be proclaiming. The direct opposite of reality.

It isn't all misery; you get to be right about something for a change. You know what is true while everyone around you lives in a hazy fog of lies. If it isn't appealing to you yet, here is the selling point. You lose all fear. After all, reality is pretty much the scariest thing, worse than death in my opinion. However, reality leaves a lot of questions for us followers to answer.

Which leads us to my hometown of Clermont, Wisconsin. If you haven't heard of it, that's fine. It sort of got sucked into the rest of the state by being unimportant by society's rules. It's a little town without much to do, but it does have somewhere to go. The suicide bridge.

An Aokigahara of our own. After the cutting fails to bring relief and the drugs wear off, these hopeless souls find themselves teetering on the edge of a rough wooden rail before succumbing to a river that loathes them. It sounds peaceful at first mention but trust me, I've seen it firsthand and it's a gruesome horror.

Yes, I come here a lot. Not to die but to think about death. We chase after dreams that we create and long for, only to run closer to our final days. Allow me to explain this better. The suicide bridge isn't finicky. It takes all ages, all genders, all races, and all lives. Sleeping quietly under the sun, it roars at night, devouring its victims. It has no enemy, no lifespan, and no escape.

But it does offer a choice. I've stood on that railing, asked myself how much I want to die, and clambered back to the safety of firm planks beneath my tingling feet. The mind is the real murderer here. The bridge, well, it's just the accomplice that's left with all the dirty work.

What brings a person to the point of self-destruction? That could be a lot of things such as criticism, a rough childhood, or broken relationships. The list goes on to infinity with different attributes for everyone. Your story is only as private as you allow it to be. Force back the tears, wear long sleeves, and use the darkness, whatever it takes. Or tell it all to someone you trust: your family, the world. It's a choice given to all.

Pride goes before a fall they say. In this case, it is literally true. We tend to trick ourselves into believing we can solve our own problems when honestly, the real problem is ourselves. Naturally we fail. You can't change who you are after all. Then we look for help in the monotone psychiatrist, hypnotics, drugs, doctor visits, alcohol, friends, and family. The list could go on forever. But people leave, money runs out, veins die, and the bridge beckons.

Names etch themselves on our hearts, so the bridge likes to collect those with our souls. Look at the wooden planks of the bridge and carved or painted on them are the awful titles given to its victims which they left behind as a legacy. Liar, freak, atheist, loser, whore, traitor, slut, lazy, pathetic, depressed, psychopath. Who gives these people the power to name us?

Now this has all just been a drive-by glance at how my fascination with the bridge began, why people levitate to it so eagerly. But now that we are more acquainted, let's move on. Perhaps I should add some history for good measure. Of course, that means shining a light on Melissa Downs, the first named victim of the suicide bridge.

1

Melissa Downs was pretty, the way leaves are in the fall. Too hard of a breeze seemed capable of knocking the girl down she was so frail. Her days consisted of early morning walks through the park which ended up at the bridge. There she let the sunlight dapple her porcelain skin while she painted the bridge in all its morbid beauty for the hundredth time.

She was often called Goth for her art with all of its dark hues, harsh lines, and random silhouettes. Actually, though, they were blind, while she had the eyes of the world and of the broken. Those lost people who gave up their bodies to the water; she was painting their final ends as a means of paying respect.

At thirteen years old, she was threatened with sexual assault at her public school. She came home in a burst of tears with her clothes torn and her skirt damp with traces of sticky blood.

"H-he came after me," she stammered hysterically. "I told him no, no, no..."

"Who, Melissa?" her mother demanded. "Who came after you?"

Melissa raised puffy red eyes to her mother's disgusted visage. "Asher Baine. He said since my skirt was shorter than the other girls', I must be a whore so he treated me like one. He...he..."

She broke off in a fit of sobs, choking for breath as her body shook uncontrollably. By now her father had also heard the raucous and joined his wife in the kitchen. "What is going on here? Pull yourself together, Melissa."

"He raped me!" she screamed. It was like a scab being torn off. Her voice was so raw, revealing the wound which had poisoned her soul.

"That damn short skirt."

"What?" She stared at them in disbelief. "I was raped. RAPED! And all you can say is my skirt was too short?"

Her father sighed and sat down in the mahogany dining chair. "Look, we aren't necessarily saying it was all your fault, but you do love attention. You always have to be number one, isn't that right? So maybe, and I am not saying for sure, but maybe you led him on without even realizing it."

Melissa continues to shake but not from the sobs, from the rage boiling to the surface within her. She, a thirteen-year-old girl, had been raped by a sixteen-year-old boy with a disgusting mind. True, her skirt was short but that was only because her legs were so long, not because she was a slut.

It had happened after the last period. The rest of the day had gone surprisingly well, although she did notice him looking at her more than boys usually did. Finally, after the last bell, he approached her outside the school by the back entrance.

"Your mind is insane, but I could get past it," he cajoled her, slouching against the brick building.

Melissa's heart rate quickened as her fingers fumbled at the lock securing her bike. She knew she had to get out, knew Asher was a terrible person, knew she was in danger. But she had to stall, do or say anything, to buy herself some precious time.

"I, um, my aunt says I'm intellectual." Inwardly she kicked herself for saying something so stupid. All she could come up with was a nerdy comment to make herself sound stuck up.

"Ah, think you're a cut above the rest of us, do you?" He came closer until she could smell the marijuana mingled with stale smoke. "What if I just laid you down right now and showed you something books ain't going to teach you?"

Melissa knew what was coming, knew it was futile to run. Despite her slender frame, she was anything but athletic and could never outrun him. So she spat in his face.

Slowly, as if in disbelief, he raised a hand to wipe the saliva from his face. Then, with lightning speed, he slammed her against the wall, tearing her shirt open down the front. With a hunger that frightened her, he grabbed at her bra, ripping it from her while her back stung in protest at the sudden tension. She began to cry then, softly at first which turned into loud wails. He glanced up from undoing her belt, punching her hard against the jaw. "Shut up or you get it harder next time."

Squeezing her eyes against what she knew was to come, he ripped off her skirt with rugged force before kicking her to the gritty asphalt. Next came off her underwear, but all she noticed was her glasses. Fallen from her narrow face with the chaos, they'd been smashed. Nothing was pure anymore, everything was spoiled.

Asher proceeded to clamor on top of the poor girl, forcing himself inside of her until her screams sounded more animal than human. He went in and out over and over and over until she began to bleed. She was quieting down, succumbing to the initial pain of releasing her virgin state to this monster.

He pressed her shoulders down into the asphalt. She focused on each individual rock being pressed into her skin, every cut that leaked her blood. His legs felt heavy on her own, twisting her ankles into sore contortions. She thought the worst was over until he grabbed a handful of her hair and pressed his lips to her own.

In a breathless state of panic, she attempted to fight him off as she gasped for oxygen. He forced his tongue into her mouth, biting her lip until a large bleeding welt formed. With his mouth still covering her own, he squeezed her breasts painfully, twisting them just to make her cringe. Melissa could swear she felt him smile at her misery. Just when she thought she would end up dead from the ordeal, he let her free and stood up.

"Tell anyone about this," he warned her, spitting on her broken form, "I'll make sure you end up dead in some ditch."

For a long time after, she just lay there in defeat. Every ounce of willpower had been sucked out of her body, leaving a shell on the pavement. Her legs felt sticky from the mucous, sperm, and blood, but she pulled her skirt up over it anyhow. Bruises colored her arms, legs, breasts, and neck. Her sweater was torn, so she used the sweatshirt, thankfully still in her backpack, to cover herself with.

Shaking, Melissa walked her bike home, too weak to ride it properly. She wanted to cry, needed to cry, yet no further tears came. Perhaps there was no exact emotion. Not fear, not sadness, anger, hate, pity, just nothing. No emotion because now she was left in shreds. Her identity had been stripped away by a teenage boy who used a gifted student for his own pleasure.

A fierce snap of her mother's fingers brought Melissa back to the present reality. "Don't be slow, listen to me!" she scolded. "You don't tell anyone about this okay? God only knows what we will do if you're pregnant."

Melissa believed deep down that she wasn't pregnant. While he had been fully inside of her, he was sloppy and the sperm had only dirtied her skin. No child would need to suffer the pains of today's miseries she hoped.

Despite the hope burning like a flame, she had known deep down what the reaction would be. Her parents didn't care about her pain, or a young child growing up with a single mother. All that mattered was society. What would their friends think of their pathetic, raped daughter of thirteen years of age having a child? The horror of it all.

Every month, sometimes several times a month even, they would throw extravagant parties. Handcrafted alcoholic drinks would be served on silver trays; appetizers, loud music, gossip, the works. Melissa would wait on her parents' friends all night long, forced to wear gaudy clothes which they told her were the latest trend. It was better than her dusty librarian wardrobe, they informed her tactlessly.

Every night after the last guest left around three o'clock in the morning, she would curl up on the floor by her bed and cry herself into a dreamless sleep devoid of pain.

In the morning, a shower of icy water washed the last night's tears away, clearing the red dots and puffy eyes. Her parents were naturally hungover so she was allowed to eat in peace without being told she was fat and shouldn't. Everything was about appearance in their eyes. Even so, how corrupt could these two individuals be to not notice the ruinous state of their daughter before them? Melissa knew nothing she said now could possibly alter their minds. They'd made their decision whether she chose to accept it or not.

Wordlessly, she grabbed her bag from the steel table in the foyer, limping painfully up the twisting staircase. Her room seemed almost foreign, like entering a world entirely new. Posters of uplifting quotes from authors smothered the walls, claiming truths that proved to be lies in her now broken mind. Her legs could no longer bear the weight of standing, so she stumbled over to sit on the edge of her bed. A small stain of crimson blossomed from her skirt onto the fluffy white comforter. Insanity overtook her, allowing a stream of laughter to burst forth out of her.

With the stark contrast of red on white, the stain would never be permanently gone. It would haunt her, yes, but her parents would be completely furious over the imperfection. Anything less than perfect was nothing to them, hence their relationship to their daughter.

It was a choice to fight or die. So shrugging off her sweatshirt, skirt, and undergarments, she made for the shower. She needed to feel something, anything, just to know she was alive. The burning water scalded her skin, turning it red with heat. The small cuts on her flesh prickled violently, but she only relished the pain, scouring at her thighs to remove any memory of the day's events.

Without her consent, tears once again leaked from her eyes. It all was so unfair, so wrong, so...soon. Melissa had first gotten her period seven months prior, leaving her self-conscious about topics regarding sexual activity. Never in all her thirteen years did she think she would get such a graphically personal representation of what it could look like, or rather, what it could *feel* like.

Long after her body was clean, she continued to let the water pour down in a cascading wave of purity. The air outside the shower bit her like an icy wind, so she pulled several towels off the rack.

Bruised, aching, and exhausted, she chose oversized pajama pants to match a faded sweatshirt two sizes too large. Her breasts, covered in teeth marks to compliment the purple swelling, were too tender for a bra so she went without. There wasn't much chance of leaving the bedroom anyhow in her current condition. If the world kicks you out, why not linger in the shadows?

2

Usually, the beginning of October was a pleasant time. The thrill of fall arriving and the leaves shining in brilliant colors, cold walks in the woods, animals busying themselves for winter. Melissa's window offered a view of an especially large maple tree, halfway between copper brown mingled with yellow hues. A few ravens rested on the branches before flying away suddenly.

Rising from her cove of pillows, Melissa crossed the room to open the window. Frigidly cold air flooded the room, turning her nose pink. She breathed in the clean scent for several moments before grudgingly closing it. The lens of her backup glasses had steamed up, so she set them on her nightstand to defrost.

It was Friday, a day she often despised but now cherished. A weekend without seeing him, the monster.

How could she ever return to that school? Terror shook her body at the fear of going through it again.

No, that was never going to happen. Not if she had any power in the matter. She'd take a knife or something, anything, to defend herself with. A second time around could render her dead, or worse, pregnant. Yet what if she was? The thought flitted in and out of Melissa's thoughts, torturing her relentlessly with the notion that she may be with child. At thirteen years old, what kind of life could she give to it?

Tomorrow morning she would go into town for a pregnancy test. She had money, so at least she did not need to beg her parents. Most likely there was nothing to worry about, but a piece of mind didn't hurt. Settling down amongst several pillows with her grandmother's old quilt draped carelessly over her legs, Melissa drifted off to a deep sleep devoid of any nightmares from the day.

When the morning dawned, sunlight announced a clear blue sky with no clouds in sight. It was too perfect. The world was a dark place now, where no light could ever thrive again. Death couldn't even enter into this dark realm, for it was a void of emptiness. A steady ache had settled into the young girl's bones. Only one thought kept her alive, got her up and out of bed. It was the urgent question of pregnancy.

True, Melissa loved children; their wide-eyed innocence, acceptance, unconditional love, and sweet laughs. She loved them so much that she would not permit herself to bring a child into the world when she herself was a dependent. It would only lead to a life of adversity.

It was a half mile to the drugstore where she intended to pick up the tester. Pulling on a pair of thick socks to accommodate a pair of warm boots, she left the house to get answers. But what would the cashier think? It was a prideful, meaningless thought. Yet it haunted her all the same. There was always the option of theft. The mere idea set her nerves on edge, the hair on her neck standing up in alarm. However, she did not dismiss the possibility of such an opportunity.

Keeping her head low, she entered the store feeling like a convicted criminal. It was easy to find the section she sought as the pharmacy was small. She chose the cheapest one which would still show results. Then stuffing it deep in her pocket, she left the store with no witness to capture her act of deviousness. For all her faults, Melissa was honest. In her schoolwork, home life, with any jobs she held, honesty was a priority. Even her virtues, simple as they may be, were stripped away from her, leaving her a corpse for the vultures of society's slums.

The deed was done. Melissa dug her fingernails into the soft palm of her hand until beads of blood studded the surface. Stepping into a gas station, she quickly ducked into the women's restroom, tearing the small tester from its store packaging. Clumsily, she tried to follow the instructions, feeling as though more urine ran onto her hand than the soft tip of the stick. Following step three, she laid it horizontally on the tile floor, watching the lines in the little circular window.

Without even bothering to wash her hands, she waited. The sheet showed that one straight line meant no pregnancy; in the clear. A cross of lines forming a plus sign, however, meant that a child was already forming in her uterus. Time stood still. There was no sound, no life, nothing. Her heart fell to her stomach in disbelief. At thirteen years old, Melissa Talia Downs was pregnant.

She stumbled out of the restroom, not bothering to throw away the mocking test stick still resting casually on the floor. There was no more future for her now, any lingering dreams destroyed. Her family would shun her for sure, or worse, make her life even more tortuous.

It was not right, she did not ask for this, nor had her child. Her child. The words rattled in her brain like foreign invaders. This was all a bad dream. All of it wasn't real, wasn't real, wasn't real....

But it was real. In nine months she would be a mother to a newborn infant who was solely dependent on her. And what of the child's father? If he didn't die of a drug overdose would he win custody and eventually come to rape her own baby? Thoughts of Asher Baine beating her unconscious and taking her child, no, *their* child haunted her mind. She couldn't allow that, could she? Was there yet time to fix one wrong out of hundreds of others?

Only one place would welcome her. The suicide bridge. With open arms, it would envelop her; drag her and the child to safety where no one would ever be able to judge her again. Without thinking, she started to walk to the bridge. Approaching the railing, she raised one foot over the other until she stood teetering on the top. It was higher than she'd imagined, although she had always been afraid of heights. The wind whipped at her clothes, urging her closer to the edge of the abyss, where only air and darkness could remain.

Closing her eyes against a swell of tears, she prayed for forgiveness. She was a broken, awful person, not even human anymore. Just a creature of ugly truths brought to the horror of reality. So, arms stretched out like a bird of song, she swooped off the edge, the impact of the water knocking all breath from her lungs. Cold slowed her blood, making everything seem softer; her thoughts furry around the edges as though in a haze.

In her youth, she had forgotten to weigh herself down with stones, but there was no will left in her to fight. Blowing a stream of miniature bubbles to the surface, she let the water fill her body to drag her farther and farther to its depth. Her throat felt constricted in a vice as her lungs futilely tried to rid themselves of the water. Spasms shook her small frame as the life left her.

The last thought that passed through the mind of thirteen-year-old Melissa was how beautiful the view had been before she leaped, and how much her old self would have enjoyed painting it.

3

Was that the first victim ever to be swallowed by the recesses of the bridge? No, she was not. Many had gone before, but the water had a supernatural tendency to steal not only their lives but any lingering trace of their identity.

Similar to a vortex, it spirals farther than just the individual succumbing to its power. Rather, it consumes all the family, friends, even the mere acquaintances who knew that person. Their memories become slurred until that person is nothing more than the fake smile they flashed for their last glossy photograph.

For the case of Melissa Downs, her identity disappeared almost entirely. No one remembered her; hardly even her rapist. Only one soul felt any emotion to her death. That one soul was Thomas Dendricks. He was in her class, sat in the back opposite corner from her, but never spoke.

She was the star student, perfect grades, reading at senior level, always asking for extra credit assignments. Whereas Thomas struggles with severe dyslexia marred by even worse headaches. There was no way anyone could see potential in him, so why even try? Melissa Downs was far too good for him, but it didn't stop his feelings from growing stronger.

His family is supportive. Since the first grade, they funded special classes or group play days so he could interact with kids like himself without fear of being teased. Their efforts meant well. The *special* children didn't tease him, but he was still able to be hurt. Once, in third grade, Thomas overheard the special needs teacher speaking to his dad.

"Thomas doesn't even play," she had openly complained.

"He is trying his best," Allen Dendricks explained patiently. "Elise and I weren't able to have other children so...it has always been just Tom. It's a new situation."

"It has been over a year now," she snapped suddenly. A few children had glanced up at the rise of volume in her voice, so she spoke in fast whispers. "How do you know he isn't retarded? I have worked with children who have disabilities for my entire career and he's a strange case."

Allen regarded her coldly. "What are you insinuating?"

"I want him gone."

There was no arguing, no swearing or threats. His father simply went over to kneel by Thomas, speaking cheerily to him in low tones. "Hey, Tommy, want to go get some ice cream?"

Even at his young age, he understood that his father meant to bribe him. "Don't I have another hour here?"

Allen ran a hand through his thinning hair, wishing for once that his son was not so perceptive. With a deep breath, he tried a new tactic. "Nah, it's kind of lame here, isn't it? Let's go do something more fun."

Thomas figured it was futile to argue, knowing that his father had his mind set on leaving. To be honest, he had heard every word of the exchange between his father and the teacher. It hadn't fully sunk in yet, so he was buying time to decide how to feel about it all.

There was no mystery to be solved here. For his entire life, he'd been diagnosed as the special child, one who could not function at the same speed as other children or who became distracted by the slightest object of interest.

It was not a mental condition, however, but actually a personal choice. He believed that the other children his age were behind him when it came down to intelligence. What would benefit the future? Some petty playground game with boys against girls, acting like toddlers? Or deep thinkers who pondered the world at large?

Thomas was young, but he knew how corrupt the world was. His aunt had committed suicide just two years ago, leaving a ghost of his mother behind in her grief. The details were vague, something about a bridge, his distant uncle, and a cold night. His curiosity burned within him, but he had no courage to inquire about the matter.

Allen laid a hand on his son's frail shoulder, snapping Thomas out of his reverie. "It'll be all right," he sighed deeply as though not believing his own lies. "There is absolutely nothing different or weird about you, okay, buddy? That teacher is just full of nonsense."

Cringing inwardly, Thomas nodded. He felt it like a personal insult. His mother had sunk into depression after his aunt committed suicide, so everything he did or said could set her off at a moment's notice. Every night he would play through all the regrets circulating in his mind of everything he had ever messed up. It was masochistic but also a coping mechanism.

The wooden steps of the old schoolhouse creaked ominously as the pair descended them. It was a pleasant walk home with maple trees flanking the street, brick houses properly maintained, and a crisp scent to the air. Yet everything was subdued by the reality of the bridge they had to cross.

That infamous suicide bridge. It crossed the wide stream, or rather river, with no way around it. Climbing higher up it, his father stared directly ahead with eyes of steel. Thomas chose to take it all in. The dark surface of the water, rough wooden railings leaning slightly out as though beckoning him to join his aunt. Sometimes he thought he heard whisperings, pleas from the lost souls who found no other escape but death. That was nonsense, though, and he knew it. Well, sort of, but it did get tough to always distinguish reality from his mind's world.

After they crossed the last foot of the bridge, his father breathed a sigh of relief. Thomas looked up at him, brown eyes wide with curiosity at what troubled his father so. The bridge was like a friend he thought, guiding those whose time was up to the other side. It was these paranormal thoughts that drove people away from him. In preschool he tried to find ghosts in the brick schoolyard, earning himself the term *possessed* by several parents. After he was politely asked to leave that school, his parents homeschooled him for the remainder of the year until first grade rolled around.

Then he attended a more prestigious school where he was informed there was no supernatural activity whatsoever to concern himself over. He believed otherwise but bit his tongue to please his parents. Thus, blending in became his power. No one could expel him if he went undetected. Teachers respected his study habits, his perfect attendance, and quiet demeanor. During any minute of free time, though, he was listening. Listening to the whispers all around him. A choir of the dead calling out their last wishes, hopes, regrets. Was it all just in his head? Was he clinically insane?

It was tedious to attend the sessions arranged for him with his psychiatrist. At the end of the day, those therapeutic talks were a tangled mess of lies to avoid further questioning. No one really cared anyhow. Thomas really wanted help. To them, it was just another client to tally on the paycheck.

The fact that his parents *did* care was touching, though. They always went out of their way for their only child. He never rode the bus, was given gifts for every occasion, and loved beyond measure. It was a life of fantastical bliss if you left out the disability. Being old enough now, though, and with the skill of hiding the unpleasant effects it could have, he almost felt normal in society. True, there was the title of nerd still floating around but for the most part, he was fitting in.

Hunting around in his jeans pocket, his father eventually locates the house key with the braided yarn adornment that Thomas had made his parents as a toddler. It is misshapen, dusty, fraying at the edges but still, they refuse to take it off. Their only concern was who had made it and much they love the artist behind the craft.

Thomas scuffs his shoes under the oak table in the entryway, following the scent of cookies to the kitchen where his mother is busily baking and frosting several batches of pumpkin-shaped cookies.

"Thomas!" she smiles warmly, tiny crinkles branching out around the corners of her hazel eyes. "You're home early, honey. Did you have a nice time?"

He picks up a cookie from the cooling rack, slowing crumbling the edge before testing it. The soft buttery flavor warms his tongue, filling him with comfort. "I don't have to go back," young Thomas spoke around the sweet. "Dad said the teacher is full of nonsense anyway."

Tangible silence seeps into the room before an explosion of chaos. "I'm sorry!" Thomas blurts out, wishing he hadn't snitched. "I didn't...I would never..."

"Allen, why can't you control your emotions?" Elise slams her hand on the counter passionately.

"I didn't mean to. You should have heard the teacher," Allen stammers defensively. "She told me he can't come back, Elise. Our son isn't allowed to go there anymore because according to that *teacher*, our son doesn't play right."

All the fight drains out of Elise as she realizes the depth of her husband's words. "Hey, Tommy, why don't you go read in your room for a bit honey."

Grabbing two more cookies to go, he heads obediently upstairs. But he doesn't read like his mother suggested. Instead, he presses an ear to the heat vent, therefore catching every word of the conversation being played out downstairs.

"I'm going to enroll him in that prestigious school on the east side of town."

"Edelton?" Allen asks incredulously. "The tuition..."

"We will find a way," Elise concludes stubbornly.

Now sitting in his advanced English literature class, thirteen-year-old Thomas is still ashamed of how he got to go to such an outstanding school. A disability, lack of involvement with his peers, pity from his parents; it makes him feel like a charity case.

There is a chair in the back row at the left corner. Nail scratches riddle the cheap plastic surface from the girl who used to reside there. For an instant, he can picture her. Long legs ironic to her slight frame. Delicate thin hands twisting her raven black hair into anxious knots. She was the nerd of the class but to him, no one would ever be more perfect.

Now she is gone. He'd gone to the bridge several times that week since her death, but she wouldn't talk to him. Maybe everyone was right. Maybe there is no special ability to communicate with the dead, only hallucinations in the demented mind of a thirteen-year-old child. There is no point to life. Melissa had killed herself because of that very reason. People leave you, or you hurt them when they stay. There is no in-between, no perfect relationships, no happiness.

Thomas knows that he has found his purpose, though. Asher was guilty, there is no doubt. Thomas had heard her screams rip through the air, heard her rapist's sadistic laugh, saw the girl ride away with her skirt smeared in that devil's semen.

Still, he remained as aloof as ever, much to his own self-disdain. Every day he wakes up and asks himself what he could have done differently. Would there have been time to run for help? Or attack Asher? To follow her home to see if she needed to talk?

That is what makes people hate death. They love life ironically, even though it just keeps hurting you by giving you hope. Yet hope is what the world feeds upon and it's the one thing death deprives them of. Once someone is gone, nothing can bring them back. Your hope is gone.

4

Thomas vowed the day of her death that he will bring her justice. If not justice, he will pay his debt. It has been exactly one week to the day since Melissa Downs lost her virginity on the asphalt outside the school to that cruel monster. Let them know that their school kept secrets.

The bell rang for the dismissal of school. He slowly stood up, carefully placing each individual book in his bag. Asher is laughing with several of his bawdy friends, swearing every two words they spoke. It is as if nothing is different according to him.

Alarm shoots through his mind. Was she the first? Maybe the first to die, but who else has he raped? "Didn't I tell you all along?" mocks the voice of a young woman in his ears. "But you never listen...never listen...never... listen..."

"Yes, I do!" He screams out loud. Everyone turns to face him, some in horror and others out of humor. The teacher walks briskly over and takes his arm firmly.

"What do you mean, Thomas?" Professor Andrews questions.

"I'm sorry," he mumbles apologetically. "I didn't mean it."

"Didn't mean what, Thomas?"

"To speak out loud."

"Was anyone else talking?"

"Yes." Thomas raises his eyes defiantly.

Professor Andrews steps back slightly at the confidence in Thomas's voice. "What do you mean? I heard no one but you at that moment."

"She doesn't want anyone else to hear her," Thomas confesses, immediately regretting it.

"If you mean those ghosts the shrink said you hear..." He runs a hand through his thinning hair. "Get out of my classroom and come back tomorrow with this nonsense gone you hear me?"

Thomas simply nods in agreement before dashing out of the room to catch up to Asher. What he intends to do is yet undecided. The moment has arisen with impulsive instinct being the only option available. Now the frail thirteen-year-old boy is stalking a sixteen-year-old rapist.

"Hey," he steps boldly forward, dismayed to see a smug smile growing on Asher's face. "I know it was you who killed her."

Asher stifles a laugh, then lets it burst out in pure joy. "Kill her? I didn't kill her; I just showed her what she could have." He smiles evilly. "Or rather, what she *could* have had. Guess it's too late for the little girlie now, huh?"

Something snaps inside of Thomas. Whether it be rage, guilt, grief, or longing, everything becomes chaos. There is no beginning to the problems, and there certainly will never be an end. Life doesn't box itself up with a pretty red bow to ship off any unwanted adversities. If anything, it only sends more our way.

"You animal," he spits. "She was nothing to you, just a weak young girl with innocent beauty, but you couldn't leave anything pure...no, of course not. Everything about you is abhorrent."

"Well...look at that. Seems to me I just found the dead girl's nerdy boyfriend." He shoves a hand into Thomas's shoulder, sending him staggering backward. "You want to be next, little boy?"

"Go ahead and try," he counters.

With lightning speed, Asher punches Tom in the jaw, knocking out a tooth in a spurt of blood. "Say that to me again, and I'll show you more blood."

He leaves Thomas leaning against the cold metal of the lockers, holding his tender jaw while a trail of blood drips onto his chin. It is the end of the day anyhow so he decides to risk it and just go home to clean up.

The bitter wind pushes him home, forcing the air from his lungs. Despite the uncomfortable environment, Thomas still prefers the longer route which crosses over the bridge. At least then he can be closer to her, his lost love gone forever.

Crusted blood is already beginning to shed from his skin when he reaches his house. He's over half an hour late, and his mother is watching at the window for his return. She darts to the door to open it with a pale hand clamped over her mouth in shock.

"Tommy!" she whimpers pitifully. "What did they do to you?"

Thomas starts to walk towards her open arms but stops short only ten inches away. His mother's face was a picture of defeat blended with hurt at her son's coolness. But this has to stop. This torture of always being perfect, staying silent, and blending in has to stop once and for all.

"No, mother, *they* did not do this. I am not some weakling that can't defend myself and allows myself to get beat up in the halls!" Thomas sees his mother start to open her mouth either to scold him or counter his new claim.

"Remember Melissa? Melissa Downs? Of course not, and see that's just it, no one does. And you wanna know why? Because no one knew she existed! She just blended in like a ghost, which I guess she is now. Well, guess what? From here on out, everything will be different because different is..." He struggles to find the right words and comes up with only one. "Amazing."

Elise just stares at her son for several moments in a failing attempt to understand what just transpired. "I don't know what to say," she finally admits.

Thomas's shoulders sag a little more than usual at her choice of words. "You could say that you'll support me for starters."

"Support you in *what*, Thomas?" she snaps bitterly. "Support this new 'you' that seems to only want to break rules. Being kind is more important than standing out to be popular."

"You just don't get it!" Thomas screams. He feels the heat building behind his eyes as the world begins to tilt and blur. A rock lodges itself in his throat until even swallowing is impossible. Taking a shaky breath, he blinks rapidly to clear up his emotions. His voice cracks, "Do not ever tell me what it is I want. I know myself far better than anyone thinks. Being popular? Screw being popular. I don't care about myself, is that not clear to you yet? Melissa is not the only victim of rape, but we continue to turn away because it's too crude for our perfect little lives. But that ends today. IT ENDS!"

At the end of his outburst, Thomas finds himself shaking uncontrollably but feeling freer than ever. His mother has turned to stone. When she finds her voice, it is like a stranger speaking to him. "You did not know her, Thomas. How do you know she did not ask for it and then realized it was more than she'd been able to handle?"

"What are you insinuating, mother?" Thomas's voice has become dangerously quiet.

Elise doesn't even hesitate to answer. "She was a thirteen-year-old girl, Thomas. Asher is a sixteen-year-old boy. There is a very good chance that she has, sorry, *had* a crush on him and made sexual advances. Her parents said she always dressed to show more than enough skin."

"Her parents are jerks."

"Thomas Lucas Dendri..."

"No! Why is she the only one to blame? Why is it never the actual rapist who gets some blame but just the girl?" His anger gives way to sarcasm as he realizes what everyone must be thinking of Melissa. "Oh wait, that's right. A thirteen-year-old, skinny girl, who never even talked in class, forced a dumb jock to rape her. I forgot, sorry, rapists are America's heroes."

"What is wrong with you?" His mother shouts in his face.

31

"Nothing is wrong with *me*," Thomas speaks evenly. "Forget it. This is getting nowhere. I'm outta here."

"And where will you go?"

Thomas glances back over his shoulder, a trail of dried blood now staining his polo shirt. "Somewhere that change grows." Leaving the mystery of his words hanging in the air, Thomas walks away from the only house he has ever known. All he has is a backpack and his thoughts for company.

5

Thomas finds himself back at the suicide bridge. The boards are dry and rough against his bare hands. A sliver of wood burrows into his skin, but rather than pull it out, he pushes it in farther, grimacing from the pain as it tears at his flesh. Now that he made his speech, it is difficult to decide how to implement this movement.

"Maybe this change has to start with me first," he thinks out loud. Then the realization hits him like a flood. "I need to feel what she experienced towards the end."

Clumsily, he drops his backpack on the wooden planks, wiping his sweaty palms on his slacks. Silent tears streak down his face as he raises his eyes to the clouds. "This is for you, darling."

His limbs have turned to lead as he clambers up onto the railing. Teetering on the edge of a bridge is the riskiest feat he has ever undertaken, but love gives you courage.

It is that undying love which sends him face first into the dark waters below.

The coolness of the water soothes his broken lip. Then his lungs begin to burn with an intensity he didn't know was possible. Still, he has to experience this so he pushes himself to go even deeper. Now his entire body feels like it is about to explode. Panic seizes him, so he lets out a stream of air to force himself back to the surface.

Every breath feels like a miracle despite his racing pulse. Slowly, Thomas swims to shore where he collapses in a heap, every muscle in his body shaking. To know that Melissa could handle such agony but not life torments his thoughts. There is no peace in drowning. The beauty he imagined her seeing is nothing but an illusion conjured by the dying.

"Why did you do this to me, Melissa?" he sobs into the sodden earth, smashing his fists against gravel until he sees blood smeared on his skin. "How could you leave me without saying goodbye?" Sometimes it is the inability to say goodbye to those we love that hurts the most.

His clothes are soaked now, and the weather has a definite chill to it. Thomas decides to find a place to change into dry clothes as he, fortunately, keeps a spare change in his bag. Walking aimlessly, he comes to a small gas station that looks as though it has seen better days.

A teenage girl stands behind the counter inspecting her jet black nails. Her hair is pixie cut and bleached so light it is nearly white to match her pale complexion. Black eyeliner emphasizes grey eyes that seem to see everything at once. Rather than greet Thomas or ask about his bag, she just stares him down like a lion to its prey.

"I'm, uh, I'm gonna just..." Thomas holds up the backpack while his clothes drip water, evidently insinuating he has to change his clothes but too bashful to come out and admit it.

The clerk rolls her eyes and sighs quietly. "What were you even doing? Trying to join the Downs girl?"

Thomas perks up like he was electrocuted. "What do you know about Melissa?"

She backs up slightly. "Not much...just that I was working the day she came in."

"Wait, um, what's your name?" He tries to read her name tag, but it looks like someone covered it in black sharpie.

"Jas."

"Okay, Jas. So let me get this straight, you saw Melissa when you were working, right?" Jas nods solemnly. "What day was it?"

"That was Friday, the day...ya know, the day she died." Jas picks a fleck of polish off her nail and chews her lower lip. "I'm really sorry, by the way, about it all. She was pretty special to ya, huh?"

Thomas laughs without any humor. "That obvious, huh?"

She smiles sadly. "Yeah, it sort of is. Trust me, though, I didn't know her and I sure don't know you. All I know about her is based on her results and the obituary."

"What do you mean by *results*?" Thomas cannot help but feel his hopes rise at the thought that maybe, just maybe, this will lead to another clue about Melissa's demise.

Jas looks downright uncomfortable. "Um, well, it is personal but...you seem to be pretty straight so..." She closes her eyes momentarily as if to prepare herself for the words to come. When at last she is able to speak, her words tumble over each other. "It was a cheap pregnancy test. I only know that because I checked the bathroom after her and it was still there, all wet on the tiles. She was in there forever, over ten minutes I'd say. So after she, I mean Melissa, left, I, of course, went to the bathroom. That freakin' test was still on the floor in a pool of urine. I guess the poor girl didn't know how to use it since she's younger and stuff. Not that I know how, of course." she added hastily.

Thomas doubts that last bit of information but decides not to push it. There is still one last thing he is dying to know. "Well? Was she, what did..." He couldn't bear to ask the question deliberately.

"Yeah," Jas's voice cracks slightly. "The girl was pregnant."

Thomas feels as if the floor falls out beneath his feet. Melissa was pregnant. That monster really did it. He didn't just murder one girl, no, he had to take *two* lives. What is wrong with the world? How could anyone like Asher even live with themselves?

"I want him to pay," Thomas growls.

"You and me both, kid." Jas sighs. "So you grilled me, now my turn. What's your name?"

"Thomas Dendricks."

"How did you get to know Melissa?"

Tom scuffs his shoe on the tile floor, leaving a thin line of water that turns a murky brown. "That is the worst part, Jas. I didn't know her. Sure, we went to the same school and had classes together, but I never could get up the nerve to talk to her." He raises moist eyes to hers and swallows hard. "You should have seen her, Jas, you should have seen her. She was an angel, but her demons spoke too loudly for her to realize just how amazing she really was. And now she's gone...and I didn't even try..."

"Quit beating yourself up, Thomas," Jas speaks softly. "You maybe can't bring her back, but you can help others like Melissa."

"Yeah, a thirteen-year-old nerd is going to change the world," Thomas retorts.

"Or maybe a thirteen-year-old nerd and a sixteen-year-old Goth could change the world," she challenges.

Thomas looks at her in a new light. Yes, her appearance is a bit startling at first, but deep down she is just like every other victim of society. It is so wrong how the world tells us what we have to be, how to act, what's "in." What gives them power over us?

He smiles tiredly, but it is the first time he has truly smiled since Melissa's death. Maybe there is a speck of hope left in this world after all. "I think that sounds like a pretty good team to me."

Jas nods thoughtfully. "I get off in four hours, so do you want to meet back here?"

"Meet me at the bridge when you get out." Her expression is one of disbelief, but he waves a hand in dismissal. "Trust me, it will be better that way."

She nods hesitantly. "Yeah...yeah, okay then."

Thomas holds up his bag one more time. "Guess I'd better change then."

"Whatever ya gotta do," she says distractedly.

Thomas is slightly puzzled by her drastic mood change but decides to not worry too much about it. Once he is back in dry clothes, he decides to get a hard start on their project and leaves the store without anything other than a wave goodbye to Jas.

"We're going to save others, Melissa," Thomas whispers out loud. "You will never be forgotten in my heart, my darling."

6

Thomas knows where he has to go first, but it is a rather unpleasant visit to endure. Thomas has not seen his Uncle Benjamin since his aunt's funeral because, after her death, he turned to alcohol, and his mother basically shunned him from the family. But right now he could be the only person who knows the bridge's mystery.

Thomas hesitates with his hand raised to knock on the worn green door. Peeling paint gives way to the smell of mildew which turns his stomach. "For Melissa," he whispers before rapping twice on the door.

At least an entire minute passes before Thomas hears shuffling and what sounds like crunching glass. Then the door swings open to reveal a gruff looking man with bloodshot eyes staring at Thomas through long dark hair.

"Who are you?

Thomas swallows hard, regretting having come to this place at all. "Um, hey, I'm Thomas. Your nephew, Thomas. My mom was your wife's sister..."

"I don't need the genealogy kid, and your family has made it pretty clear that I am no longer welcome. So why don't ya just leave me be."

"Well guess what?" Heat rushes to Thomas's face as his anger takes over. How dare this man, his *uncle*, reject him so easily. "My mom basically kicked me out, too, and you want to know why? Because of another death at that stupid bridge! But I don't want to just keep looking away and ignoring it anymore, and I thought just maybe you had loved your wife enough to want to help end these suicides. But maybe you are happy she's gone after all."

As soon as the last words leave his mouth, Thomas instantly regrets it. "I'm so, so sorry..."

Benjamin raises a hand. "Enough, kid." His voice has lost its gruff edge. "I don't know what you came here looking for, but I can at least tell you right now that I loved her. I loved her more than anything in the world. When she died...well, all I wanted was revenge to try and ease the heartache a bit."

"Revenge for what?"

"Didn't your mom ever tell you? My wife, her sister, was raped."

Thomas's head begins to spin. It is all beginning to make sense now. The suicides, the rape victims, and the bridge are all connected like one giant knot. How could no one have seen this? Or did everyone already know and just decide to look away? This new information makes Thomas long to change even more.

"How, um...how did it happen?" He wonders awkwardly.

His uncle stares at a point just over Thomas's head as if the memory is so vivid it has him trapped. "She was at a group session for her depression. They usually got out around eight every Thursday night. So, it got to be around 10:30 and she still wasn't back, but the drive was only about twenty minutes." He pauses to swallow the lump growing in the back of his throat. "Anyhow, I went out in the truck looking for her and found her sitting up against her car on the pavement. Needless to say, I was shocked."

Benjamin takes a long swig of liquor. His free hand is balled into a fist as if he wants to destroy the very memory. "So then I got out and went up to her..."

He seems to choke and slams the bottle against the door jam, showering them both with glass. Golden alcohol drips down the wood in a rhythmic sequence. Benjamin balls up his hands, pressing them against his bloodshot eyes to stem the flowing tears. His breaths become so labored that Thomas fears his uncle will have a heart attack and die at that very moment.

"It's okay, really," Thomas says hastily. "This must be awfully painful for you, I don't expect..."

"Shut...UP!" Benjamin roars. He points a shaking finger at Thomas in accusation. "She deserves to be avenged, you know? And if telling some kid is the start then, yes, I will tell you what happened."

Thomas is taken aback by the outburst, but he is also in awe of his uncle's commitment to his deceased wife. He realizes that he has not answered yet and nods his head in reply.

"All right then." Benjamin takes a breath to steady his nerves. His voice softens in defeat. "To say she was a mess would understate the horror of it, Tom. That devil had torn her clothes to ribbons. He even *kept* some of her clothes.

When I found her, she was wearing nothing but her bra, underwear, and what was left of her leggings. Not only that...but they weren't even on her properly. Her bra was so tangled that one look said it hid nothing. The leggings must have been pulled so hard that the elastic snapped and ripped, and then there was the underwear..."

Thomas feels his face heating up at the discussion of female undergarments. Yet despite his own discomfort, he knows how hard it must be for his uncle to be so open about what should have been intimate between him and his wife. His beloved Helen had been used like an animal and left in scraps for the next monster to prey upon.

A definite crack in his voice signifies that the worst has not yet been told. "I...I knelt down by her, to comfort her. Or try to comfort her at least. But she was like a corpse. She wouldn't talk, wouldn't move, wouldn't acknowledge me....I was so scared that she was actually dead right then. But no, she was just...gone."

"Gone?" Thomas is confused. "Like...her mind?"

Benjamin shakes his head in frustration. "Not just her *mind*, Tom. Her whole identity had been stripped away leaving behind a shell of what she once was. She was always very timid of sex, and I never once pushed her more than she wanted to go. But this creature...this devil had been in her for who knows how long, pulling at her until the pain must have been blinding. She was too delicate for that. I mean, anyone would be.

"Anyhow, the blood on her thighs told me there might be internal damage, not to mention his sperm all over her clothes. I wanted to take her to a hospital, man, how I wanted to! But Helen said no. It was the only word she said, but it was so resolute that I just picked her up and took her back home."

Benjamin is crying profusely now and his whole body is beginning to shake. Thomas feels like his blood has been turned to lead from the guilt of making him retell such a tragedy. "Please, Uncle Ben, you don't have to do this."

"If I don't, who will? Just give me a moment here, boy."

They stand in the doorway awkwardly for several minutes. Thomas tries to block out the images from his mind before realizing how cowardly he is being. Instead, he chooses to relive those memories, see the gory horror of it all, and feel her pain. It brings tears to his eyes and his throat sticks together in misery, but he does not stop. If he turns away now, Melissa and Helen will be lost with no legacy or respect.

Benjamin clears his throat noisily. "All right...so like I said, she wanted to go home. When we got home, I drew a warm bath and cleaned her up, asking if anything hurt, but she didn't respond at all. It was like washing a ragdoll. Her eyes were glazed, her body limp, no emotion whatsoever. After that, I took her to bed and just held her." He tries to laugh but it is the saddest thing Thomas has ever heard. "I didn't sleep a wink, and I don't know whether or not my Helen did either. But I couldn't let her go, not ever again."

There is a long pause that makes Thomas think the story ends there. He tries to distract himself momentarily. You can see inside the house where cream and rose swirl wallpaper still stands, and a dried bouquet of roses long dead still rests in a dry vase. Every detail points back to his devastating loss. Then he starts talking so fast it is a challenge to follow his thoughts.

"The next morning I woke up and she was fast asleep. Guess I did pass out for a while. So I thought I would go surprise her, and I bought her some flowers and picked up some bakery in town. But when I got back, she wasn't in bed. She wasn't in the bathroom, she wasn't even home! She was...she...."

He breaks down into a fit of sobs, curling up into the fetal position right there in the doorframe. Thomas doesn't know what to do, but he can't just do nothing. He kneels down beside his broken uncle, inhaling stale alcohol and mildew. "She was at the bridge wasn't she?" he whispers tenderly.

Benjamin just nods miserably. "I saw her shoes on the bridge," his voice begins to crack again. "She was always so neat, so attentive to the little things, so special..."

Thomas pushes aside the last thirteen years of his life. He pushes away all the lies, all the half-truths, all the ignorance, and hugs his uncle for dear life. "You did your best, Uncle Ben. You cannot keep beating yourself up for this. Aunt Helen was lucky to have a husband like you. This was hard on you, too, and you kept enough composure to try and fix the damage. Do not blame yourself for what you didn't do, only focus on what you *did* do."

"Well, Tommy, you may just be the healing I need. It doesn't solve it all but...you have given me some hope." He grips Thomas's shoulder passionately with tears glinting in his eyes. He manages to choke out two more words, "Thank you."

Thomas smiles through his own tears. "Hey, my family gave me the boot, too, so I guess it's you and me now."

Benjamin gives a bark of laughter. "Well indeed it is, indeed it is."

The lightness of the mood dims as Benjamin finishes the story. "After I knew what had happened, I contacted the police. They retrieved her body, and I wish I had never looked, Tom, I wish I had looked away. You are fortunate you never had to see your little Melissa that way. They disappear, Tommy. Until all that is left is a swollen, cold shell of the person you used to love. Their eyes turn milky and they just look straight through you. It is as if the dead become alive, and we become the ghosts.

"Anyhow, they ran some tests to make sure it was my Helen, as if I couldn't tell. But ultimately it was confirmed in her obituary that she had been raped and went to the bridge for suicide." He sighs and runs a hand through his thinning hair. "What kills me is that her obituary never actually made it to the paper. They just stuffed it away with all the other suicide reports this town has seen."

Thomas perks up immediately. "The other reports? Do you know where I can find those?"

Benjamin looks at Thomas critically, and then it dawns on him. "Thomas, you may just be on to something. What if there is a sequence..."

"And what if it isn't just girls but even boys?" Thomas finishes.

"That is one messed up thought boy, but I can't dismiss it. It would be at the library that you'd find the reports, but you've got to be at least 18."

Thomas raises an eyebrow questionably at his uncle. "You seem to meet the age requirement."

Benjamin chuckles to himself. "Only by a few years, kid. All right, why don't you come inside while I clean up a bit and we can head over there together."

"Sure, Uncle Benjamin, I'd like."

His uncle smiles crookedly at him. "Now we're getting somewhere."

7

The house smells. Like, it literally is suffocating. But once again it is obvious that even after all these years, he has tried to leave it as his beloved wife had kept it. Thomas reaches out to touch one of the dried rose petals, and it turns to dust beneath his fingers. Everything has an aura of decay.

Thomas wanders into the kitchen next. Embroidered pictures preserved in dusty frames fill the dining room wall. It could be so quaint and homey, but instead, takeout boxes and half-eaten microwave dinners cover every inch of space. The only thing untouched is the dining table. It is set up for a romantic dinner for two: candles in brass holders, beautiful china plates and a little box tied in pink ribbon. Yet it is blemished by dust and neglect. A sign of what could have been a lovely evening turned to ashes and never to be recovered.

He is still staring at the little box when his uncle walks in. "I was going to give her that for our ten year anniversary. It was a ring with our birthstones on it. Topaz for her and sapphire for me. She always liked things that were linked back to us." He smiles sadly.

"I know she would have adored it, Uncle Benjamin."

"Yeah, well, too late for that I guess." He coughs several times to recover his composure. "You ready to go then?"

Despite the rather wretched conditions, Thomas wants to stay. He feels as though this home could tell him so much more than any library could ever offer. "Yes," he says rather reluctantly. "I am ready."

His uncle's car is not in much better condition than his home. Pulling a cardboard box from the trunk, he fills it with the trash covering the front passenger seat. Thomas is almost afraid to sit down and does so tentatively.

"The library is about ten minutes from here, so we will get there pretty soon," his uncle informs him. It is as though now that the story has been told, there isn't much else to talk about, and filling the space with words has become rather awkward.

"Cool," Thomas replies absentmindedly. He hunts around for something else to say. So...how do you fill your days now?" He winces inwardly at his choice of words. It sounds so accusing after all his uncle has been through.

"Drinking." The answer is point blank. "I mean, I have a job of course. Still have to pay all the bills. I currently work at the auto shop over on Sixth Street. It's a dump, so I fit in pretty well," he laughs bitterly.

"That just means you deserve to work somewhere better." Thomas is surprised at how defensive he got when his uncle began to degrade himself. But he knows it is true. His uncle deserves so much better.

"Do you really mean that?" He looks sideways at Thomas to gauge his reaction.

"I really do," Thomas meets his stare.

"Well, I used to work at a car dealership. Not exactly the most prestigious job on earth, but it was a step up from the auto shop. Then after Helen died...I just couldn't pull off the fake enthusiasm. It was impossible to act happy when the world had lost its light. So after about two weeks of me being a zombie, they let me go."

Thomas sinks into his seat, stunned by the lack of compassion in the world. "Why are people so cold?"

"Everyone is looking out for themselves and kindness is a nonprofit business."

It is a simple statement, yet it is so profound. Everyone in this world has to make a profit. All people care about is money and where they can get rich quick. Compassion and empathy have been kicked aside, but those are the morals that make us human. Without sympathy, we are like robots trying to function in a world that is black and white.

His uncle pulls up outside of the library. It opens in five minutes, so they get out of the car to wait. His uncle pulls out a cigarette and sticks it between his teeth without lighting it. He notices Thomas's suspicious look. "I stopped smoking when I married Helen, but sometimes just having one there is a comfort. Like it gives me something else to focus on. But I swear to you, I haven't lit one since my wedding day, and I will never break that promise that I made to my Helen."

Thomas realizes now that when his uncle makes a promise, he sticks to it. After all, that is the point of a promise, never to break it. His reverie is broken when he sees a librarian unlocking the door. All of his reluctance to come here is brushed aside at the thought of possibly uncovering the mystery that took his beloved Melissa's life.

The scent of dust, old paper, and coffee embraces them. This is what Thomas loves, being surrounded by the ideas and wisdom of the past. It is a refuge from the modern, chaotic world outside. It is a quiet place to reflect on who we really are.

"Follow me," his uncle is gruff again, but now Thomas understands that it is all a front to hide his vulnerability.

They go to a back room half composed of metal bookcases filled with periodicals from twenty years ago. Behind them is the microfiche and newspaper cataloging system. Benjamin sits down at one computer and gestures for Thomas to do the same. Seeing his bewildered expression, he slides a laminated instruction sheet over to his nephew. Thomas gives him a nod of thanks and returns to his task.

With each month or year entered, hundreds of articles pop up. The addition of a few keywords such as *suicide* or *bridge* reduces the search results to a more accessible pool of readings. Then a familiar name pops up that makes Thomas's stomach roil.

"Uncle...Uncle Benjamin..."

His uncle sees his distress and rises quickly to see his screen, knocking over the metal folding chair in the process. "What the..."

There is a list of articles with little locks next to them, but the names are clear to read. The name Helen Lanland stands out in the list. Each name is accompanied by the date of suicide with a brief mentioning of the bridge.

"I cannot believe it." Thomas swallows the bile rising in his throat. "No, actually, I can."

8

"How dare they keep this locked away," his uncle sighs in disgust. "Move over."

Thomas scrambles to his feet and watches in wonder as his uncle quickly goes into the control panel and unlocks the security code with a few taps of the keys. He smirks at his nephew. "I have some extra time on my hands to pursue a few hobbies."

Thomas isn't sure computer hacking counts as a legitimate hobby, but he can't deny how helpful it is in accessing the data they need so desperately. His uncle hesitates with the cursor poised above the link with his deceased wife's name. "I don't know if I can do this, Tommy." His voice is thick with emotion, his breathing sharp and ragged.

Without even thinking about it, Thomas leans over to embrace his uncle, feeling his shaky arms wrap tight around him. For several minutes neither of them speak. This is a fight that they are alone in, but it is a battle they intend to win. His uncle clears his throat and pulls back, dragging a hand over his eyes.

"I am so sorry you have to go through this, Tom. I am so sorry."

"Don't be. This has to be finished, and if you and I are the only ones prepared to fight this war, then so be it."

"You're right, kid." He smiles at his nephew then shakes his head. "I just really hope we *can* win."

He clicks the link to his wife's name and stares at the screen. They read in silence together as the author butchers the story. Thomas is in disbelief. "They make it sound like she was a slut." He quickly glances at his uncle to see if he spoke too much.

His uncle just sighs in defeat. "I feared as much. Look at this...they say she was out having an affair? That she asked them for sex and couldn't *handle* it?" His voice rises in anger. "Now they say that the act of suicide was *cowardly*? Who do these people think they are?"

"They are the cowards. Aunt Helen was stronger than they will ever know, but they don't deserve to know someone that powerful."

"You are just an artist with words, ain't you? Well, all I know is that if they'd had their identity stripped away, they would be no better. Just thinking of what she went through...." He shivers. "She deserved so much better. I should have been there, I should ha..."

"Stop." Thomas is surprised by the force of his voice. "She had you, Uncle Ben, and while she had you as her husband, she had the world. Love is the best gift any of us can ever give and you loved her with all of your heart every day. If that isn't special, then I don't know what is."

"Thanks, kid." He leans back, closing his eyes. Finally, he opens them to face the screen. "All right, next one."

The next name on the list is Dominick Shulfer. Not to be sexist, but neither of them had been expecting the next victim to be male. Scanning the now unlocked article, they find it to be nearly identical to Helen's. Apparently, Dominick was raped like the other victims of the bridge, but it appears as though it was still a male rapist.

"What in the world," Thomas breathes.

"It isn't entirely what you think, Tom. Oftentimes, a male rapist will go for another male, not out of sexual attraction but just to show dominance or to get revenge. It seems like the rapist involved here is a power-hungry devil."

The idea makes Thomas's head spin. How can someone take another person's identity just for the sake of power? It goes to show just how corrupt our world really is. "Do you think it is the same guy that raped Melissa?"

"I can't say for sure, but the articles date back to about ten years ago. It could very well be the same guy. But because our society likes to turn a blind eye, he just hasn't been caught yet."

"I wish he was dead," Thomas spat. He is taken aback by his violent thoughts, but it is true. No one that evil should be allowed to live.

"You and me both, kid. Come on, let's look at that first article."

The article his uncle refers to is dated ten years back to the month of September. It began with a female victim of rape, Alyssa Markson. Perhaps the rapist started out wanting sex with women and then began using his torture to dominate others around him.

His uncle's voice brings him back to the present. "It looks like she was raped viciously and then three days later committed suicide at the bridge. Those worthless authors, saying the teeth marks on her breasts were a sign she had taken her shirt off! As if the rapist couldn't tear her clothes off by force. What is wrong with people?"

Thomas wonders the same thing but says nothing as he reads the article himself. "She was 28 years old."

"Around the same age as my Helen."

They continue on to the next article which involves another female victim dated three months after the last incident. Kate Lexon was only 25 years old when she was attacked. Thomas reaches for a trash can to vomit into as he reads the graphic details. His uncle soothingly rubs his back despite the fact that his face is growing pale as well.

Thomas chokes out the question he fears is true, acid burning his esophagus. "She was raped in her home?"

"Yeah, it says in her bedroom. The semen was on the bedding, and her clothes were rags on the floor. Again, her breasts were covered in teeth marks but nothing else to prove the identity of the rapist." Then his uncle slams his fist down on the desk. "Look! They say she *invited* him into her home."

"Why do they keep doing this?" Thomas wonders aloud.

"Because no one wants to face the truth."

The next few victims are a mix of females and males. The stories are full of horrific details, but, every time, the rapist seems to be excused. This opens up the question of why rape cases are always handled so differently than other crimes. If it was a murder case, the murderer would surely be the offender. But in rape, it is as if the victim is the one they wish to punish, even after death.

"There's Melissa," Thomas almost screams.

"Calm down, kid." His uncle toys with the computer mouse. "Hey, Tommy, it might be better for you not to read this."

"What? You think I am going to be like everyone else and just turn a blind eye because it is too terrible to accept? She is dead! If she could endure all that, the least I can do is read her obituary."

"You are one honorable kid, Tom. I swear, this will destroy all your innocence and you'll never be the same again."

"Too late for that," Thomas mutters bitterly.

The article unfolds onto the screen and is worse than anything Thomas could have imagined. It makes it sound as if Melissa had passed a note to Asher in class asking him to meet her outside after school. The rest goes on to make her out to be a slut who continually tried to lure guys into having sex with her. The fact that he nearly ground her into a pulp on the pavement was described as being *passion*. Her jumping off the bridge to her death was considered to be a selfish act once they realized she was pregnant. It appears that the author takes pride in saying that Melissa was unwilling to face the consequences of her actions when she found that a child was growing inside of her.

"Wait a second," Thomas says. "There's a quote by him..."

Sure enough, there is a direct quote from Asher. "I can't believe this happened to her," he says. "After all the rapes in the past, I wouldn't be surprised if she had been the victim of him."

Not only was he trying to shrug off the blame from the press, but he knew about the other rapist. This was the only quote published on any of the articles, and why? His uncle points out a fact Thomas overlooked. "It is always the same author for every single article listed, but I can't access the name yet."

"Do you think there is some connection to that?" Thomas questions.

"Maybe, but it's hard to say with blame being thrown around so carelessly."

The clock on the wall informs the pair that they have been reading the obituaries for close to four hours. Thomas blinks rapidly to lubricate his dry eyes and Benjamin stretches with a sigh of misery. "Ready to go, Tom?"

"Yes." He is exhausted. "I don't know how much more I can take."

9

They walk silently back to the car together. Thomas whips around at the sound of his name being called. Jas is jogging over to meet him by the car, her white hair almost prismatic in the afternoon sun.

She stops a good three feet away from them and eyes his uncle suspiciously. Thomas tries to smooth over the awkward ridge. "This is my uncle, um, Uncle Benjamin. We were just looking through some obituaries."

She narrows her coal-lined eyes. "Thought we were gonna do that."

His uncle steps forward, making her step back. "Sorry to intrude on your plans, miss, but those obituaries are locked, so I helped Thomas get in." He kicks a stray stone with his hands in his pockets. "See, my wife got raped a while back, and I would give anything to bring her some justice."

Jas seems too stunned by how serious things became. The tension in the air is so thick you could cut through it with a knife. No one seems to know what to say or what to do, but finally Jas breaks the silence.

"So what, we're like a team now?

Thomas looks up, noticing the hope in her voice. He smiles wanly. "Yeah, we are a team now."

"So, you want to head over to the bridge maybe?" She gives him an appraising look.

Thomas looks at his uncle, whether it is all right to be separated from this family relation he just found. His uncle slaps a hand gruffly on his nephew's shoulder. "Go on, see what else you guys can think of to solve this. Maybe find some answer at that cursed bridge. Just be back before ten tonight, you hear?"

"Yes, of course." He is just shocked that he has a place to sleep tonight. After being shunned by his own mother, he had expected to wander around for the night or rough it out on a park bench. Even in the darkest times, a light will shine through.

Thomas walks away with Jas leading the way. The sound of his uncle's sputtering old car behind them reminds him of how broken everything is. It feels like the articles of rapes and suicides have only made the puzzle more complex without filling in any of the blanks. Is this just a loop of questions with no answers? But to quit would mean to give up on Melissa, and Thomas is determined never to let her go.

"How often do you think about her?"

Thomas jumps a bit as he is startled out of his reverie. "I never stop thinking about her, Jas. That's the thing, she is like a part of me now. Everywhere I look I see her face. I mistake strangers for her and when someone else sits in her

seat in class, I want to tell them to move out of her chair."
He runs a hand over his tired eyes. "It just doesn't feel real.
And then the voices..."

"What do you mean *voices?*"

"Nothing, you would never understand."

She stops with her arms folded defensively, forcing him
to face her. "Why, because I'm just some emo who would
never understand the tragedy of death? Maybe to you, I am
not even human, I don't even have feelings, right?" She is
nearly spitting the words out. "Why do you think I am like
this, Thomas? It is because I feel too much! Everything
bothers me and it is like I feel their pain. But who cares, I
guess. I mean, I don't understand anyway."

"Well, how am I supposed to know how you feel
anyway, huh?" He is livid now. His voice rips apart in a
series of screams. "No one tells me anything! Ever! All I am
is the shadow who watches everyone drift away, and there
is nothing I can ever even do. My mom just shunned me,
but I probably don't care right? Because I don't ever think
about anyone but myself, and especially I must be ignoring
poor Jas, right?"

Tears are threatening to spill from Jas's eyes, but she
wills herself not to let him see her cry. "I am not the one
who needs your pity. *You* have enough pity for yourself.
Because you were right about one thing. You only think
about yourself, Thomas."

"How can you say that?" His voice is barely a whisper,
but the rage it conveys makes Jas shrink into herself. "Every
moment I think of her, I feel her pain. I feel the gritty
asphalt being embedded in her delicate skin, and his mouth
sucking the breath from her and tearing at her pink lips.
I feel her shame and misery and at her family's reaction.

If I could, I would die her death to feel every second of suffocating pain that my Melissa felt."

"I...I'm sorry, Thomas."

Thomas turns away from her, sick again at the thought of what she went through. All her innocence torn away by the claws of that demon. Why not him? Why everyone else, but he was always kept safe, tucked away like a doll. Nothing worse than being teased had ever made his existence a burden. Yet Melissa, sweet young Melissa, had to see the horror of this world in a personal experience.

Jas shuffles uncomfortably and twists one of the many rings adorning her fingers. "So...back to these, um, voices."

"You are going to think I'm crazy, but I don't even care anymore. It has been this way since I can remember. I could be lying in bed, taking a shower, sitting in class, or eating dinner, and it doesn't matter. All of a sudden I just hear voices. Sometimes I can tell it is male voices, but usually, it is women talking. But...it isn't just the typical inner conscious nonsense that everyone wants to pass it off as. It is the whisperings of the dead."

He stares at her with a fire burning in his hazel eyes, challenging her to contradict him or tell him that, yes, he is indeed insane. Jas has stopped playing with her ring and now simply stares back at him with grey eyes widened in shock. "That isn't you being crazy, Thomas," she says softly.

"Mmm...how so?"

"Because it means you feel things on a deeper level. You look beyond the surface to see what others ignore. While the rest of the world walks around in a sort of fog, you perceive life as unending." She smiles through a mist of tears. "You aren't crazy, Thomas. You're gifted."

Thomas looks up to see the bridge before them, allowing him to dodge Jas's last comment. "We're here." He kicks himself internally for stating the obvious.

Jas isn't quite ready to ignore the subject yet. "Thomas, really, you are gifted..."

"Please, Jas," he pleads miserably. "Just drop it, all right? Some people are born freaks, but I've learned to come to terms with it.

He catches a slight spark in her eyes and realizes that in berating himself, he may also have insulted her. Yet, it doesn't bother him much since he is used to ticking people off. Nowadays, everything bothers everyone. You could compliment a stranger on their shoes and be filed for harassment. Why use a filter when the world doesn't seem to have a preference either way?

He clears his throat rather awkwardly. "So, um, this is where the voices are always strongest for me."

Jas just nods silently. It annoys Thomas how sensitive she is. "You know you're allowed to speak, right?"

"Why should I?" she explodes. "Everything I say either hurts someone or makes them angry. I try to help someone I love, and they end up hurt or worse. Nothing I do makes anything better! So if you want me to talk, then fine, I'll talk. But just know that all you are going to hear is a bunch of rubbish."

Thomas feels a twinge of guilt. He had always considered himself to be a fairly kind person, but Melissa's death and the newspaper obituaries have seriously screwed up his mind. "I'm sorry." He lays a hand carefully on her arm, feeling the soft fabric graze his fingers.

She flinches at his touch as if in pain. His face contorts in concern. "Jas, do you..."

60

"So what did you find at the library?" She pulls her sleeves farther over her wrists.

He decides to let her discomfort slide for now but cannot fully hide his concern. "Well, my uncle and I basically just looked through dozens of unpublished obituaries for hours."

"Sounds fun," she comments dryly.

"As if," Thomas spits. "Anyhow, they just kept getting worse and worse. The writer for that newspaper is a sadist. He made it sound like my Aunt Helen was asking for sex and couldn't *handle* it. Melissa apparently passed a note to Asher to meet her outside." He ignores Jas's shocked face and continues. "Some of the earlier suicide victims were said to have invited the rapist inside or said they'd been sluts. It was horrible, Jas. He wasn't just demoralizing the dead, he was shrugging any blame off the rapist."

"We have to find him."

Thomas looks over at Jas who is curled up in a ball on the bridge, only her eyes showing above her folded hands. The word 'outcast' is carved in jagged print next to her elbow. It makes Thomas wonder who wrote it and what made them feel like an outcast in society. Then again, who isn't an outcast?

Jas looks more vulnerable somehow like a strong wind could take her away. It is the first time Thomas has really looked at Jas as being a human being with feelings. He decides it is time to start being the kind person that he used to be and to stop letting the current events turn him bitter.

"How do we do that?"

She shuffles a bit to face him, still only showing her eyes. They blaze like stars in a dark sky as she tells him her idea.

"Well, first, we get his writing name. I say that because he could be writing under a pseudonym. After that, we decide whether or not that is actually his real name. Then once we know that much, we dig into his background."

"My uncle has some pretty good hacking skills."

"Now we're getting somewhere."

They sit in silence together; the only sound is the October breeze shaking dead leaves from the tree branches. It would be peaceful except for the whispers. Thomas knows that they are a long way from peace, but at least he knows that he is no longer alone.

10

They linger for a bit longer at the Suicide Bridge, just enjoying the few blissful moments of near silence. Thomas feels a tingling sensation as his legs turn numb from sitting on the rough wooden boards. He struggles back to his feet, reaching out a hand to help Jas up as well.

"So, time to execute the plan?" she asks with forced enthusiasm.

"Might as well. But before we get too carried away, I want to run our idea by my uncle if you're cool with that."

Jas shrugs indifferently. "I'd be cool with it."

It is a long walk back to his uncle's house, but he savors the chance to burn off some energy and feel the open space around them. He has been confined his entire life, and now he had been given a brief taste of freedom. It is frightening but still exhilarating.

"You sure we shouldn't just call him to pick us up?" Jas huffs after ten minutes of steady walking.

Thomas chuckles quietly. "I'm not athletic either, but I need to stretch my legs."

She picks up the pace defiantly. "I never said I wasn't athletic."

It is too much, her pompous gait and pixie cut styled hair. Then she stumbles on a crack in the road and trips into him. He can't help but laugh out loud. "Yeah, very athletic. Oh, and graceful. Very graceful, Jas."

"Whatever," Jas rolls her eyes but maintains a half smile. "Guess I better just enjoy the hike."

Their brief joking lightens the mood considerably which is a great relief to Thomas. After about twenty more minutes and a few shortcuts later, they arrive at his uncle's home. Even though it isn't even his, he has ties to the house and feels a flush of embarrassment creeping up his neck. "It is kind of run down but…"

"It's perfect," she whispers, looking down at her shoes.

Thomas glances sideways at her in bewilderment. "I don't know if I'd go so far as to say it is perfect but…"

She whirls on him. "It has hope, and there was love here once and probably still is." Tears leak from her eyes, and a trail of mascara runs down her cheek. "Really, Thomas, why are appearances so important to you?"

Jas leaves Thomas standing there in shock as she storms into the house. He has no choice but to follow her, and yet he feels as though he has just learned some sacred secret of hers.

Thomas eventually walks into the house to find Jas and his uncle talking amiably on the sagging living room sofa. There is a friendly glow about her, but he can still decipher the lingering sadness hidden inside her heart. He longs to help her, to make her feel wanted and loved, but with his own emotions so messed with, it is hard to know how to heal someone else who has been broken.

His uncle looks up at the sound of his nephew's footsteps. "Hey, Tommy, why don't you join us?" He gestures to an equally sagging armchair. "Jas has come with a pretty good plan if you want to hear it."

Jas beams with pride. She doesn't wait for Thomas's consent and merely starts talking. "So I remembered you saying that your uncle had epic hacking skills, so he's going to look into some hidden or locked files to get more information from wherever we can find it. We are going to read any documents or articles written by this mystery author.

"Then I will check out the social media side of things if he has any. You know, if he has Facebook, Twitter, whatever. Find past emails, who is he friends with, what does he follow? Quite often people post their greatest secrets in plain sight without realizing that social media is open to the public."

Once again, Thomas feels that there is much more to Jas than meets the eye. She has a bit too much experience with this, and her discomfort towards the bridge suggests a prior memory linked to it. What bothers him the most was her cringing at his gentle touch. It was natural to wear long sleeves or even a jacket in the chilly October weather, but she seemed to be in physical pain. He has some ideas about it but feels uncomfortable asking her directly.

It also surprises him that Jas is so eager to help him avenge Melissa. True, she could just be a very compassionate person, but it seems to be more personal than that. Perhaps she lost someone she loved to the bridge and hopes that by avenging Melissa, she too can find peace.

"Sounds like a good plan to me," Thomas confirms. He plasters a smile on his face in an attempt to look convincing. "When should we start?"

11

J ust then his phone rings, interrupting the conversation. It is his mom calling his cell after he has been gone for over twelve hours. A fierce battle wages inside of him as he decides whether or not to answer. After five rings, he takes the call.

"Hello?"

"Hey, Tommy," his mother's voice is sugary sweet. "I hope you're okay, baby. But I think you need to come home. You are too smart to continue this craziness."

"What craziness?" He ignores her fake concern as his anger bubbles to the surface.

She sighs in frustration, all sweetness gone. "Thomas, enough. Melissa died and that's all there is to it. You need to come home and forget about all this."

"Forget her?" Thomas asked incredulously. His voice rises steadily in volume. "I will never forget Melissa, NEVER!"

"Where are you, Thomas? I am coming to get you."

"Maybe you should take your own advice, Mom. Just forget me and stop all this *craziness*."

He hears her still talking but slams his finger on the button ending the call. Then he turns the power off on his phone and shoves it deep in his pockets. His uncle and Jas are both staring at him in shock.

Benjamin comes to first. "You are one bold kid, Tom. Melissa is lucky to have you fighting for her like this."

It lifts Thomas's heart to hear his uncle speaking of Melissa in the present tense. "Thanks, Uncle Ben." He turns to face the still quiet Jas. "We still good then?"

She nods rather hesitantly. "Yeah, we're good."

It annoys him how his mom continues to doubt his devotion to Melissa. Yet at least he can be certain that she has been thinking about him. Unlike her, his dad seems to care very little about Thomas or where he could be. It leaves him feeling small and loved, but he desperately tries to shake off the feeling.

"I know how you're feeling, Tom," Jas whispers in his ear. His uncle vacates the room, and whether it's because he thinks they are having a moment or just need space matters little.

"What do you mean?"

She shifts a bit closer, biting her lip ferociously. "When I was fourteen years old he left. It wasn't even the right kind of leaving. Like, usually the dad leaves when you're a baby, or after a big fight, but he just left us. I suppose it has to do with Lisa but what about me?" Tears flood down her cheeks as her voice cracks. "Was I just the other half who meant nothing to him? If it has been me and not her, would things have been different?"

Even after her emotional outburst, Thomas can only focus on one question. "Who's Lisa?"

"I'm not ready to talk about that yet," she refuses to meet his eyes. "Trust me, saying all I did was hard enough. You just have to believe that when the time comes I will tell you everything, but you have to be patient with me."

Thomas takes her small hand in his own. "Jas, I cannot promise you much, because I have learned all too well that promises are empty truths. But what I can promise you is that I will never push you or force you into anything that makes you uncomfortable. I will never leave you, and whatever demons you're fighting, I will fight them with you."

She stares at him in stunned silence for several heartbeats and Thomas wonders if he went too far. Then, as if on impulse, she throws her arms around his neck. He returns the embrace, rubbing her thin back over and over, more to soothe his nerves than her own. "Thank you," she sighs into his shoulder.

"Always, Jas."

They stay like that for several minutes, neither one wanting to break this moment of peace they share. It is a relief for Thomas to know he is not alone, but he wonders about the unknown burden Jas carries with her. He wants to help, but he promised not to push her or pry, so, for now, all he can do is hold her.

Just then, Benjamin enters the room and takes in the scene, noticing the emotion heavy in the air. They scoot farther away from each other as if to dislodge any ideas he might have. Thomas raises his hands to feel the heat rising in his cheeks. He has never had a sister, so girls are somewhat foreign to him.

Benjamin clears his throat noisily. "So, tomorrow is Melissa's funeral. I know you guys probably don't want to have to see her parents and, trust me, neither do I. But we aren't going for the family. We are going for Melissa."

Thomas casts a side glance at Jas and can see that she, too, realizes there is no choice in the matter. They are not being asked to go, they are being told to go. Thomas scrabbles around for an excuse not to go. "I don't have anything to wear."

Jas gives a short bark of laughter, more from nerves than from humor. "Well, good thing you currently have something to wear, or this situation might be compromising."

Thomas doesn't even smile. "That isn't what I meant. At the funeral, like, I have nothing nice to wear because all my clothes are at my parents' house."

"So we go and get it." His uncle stares at him with a determined fire in his eyes.

"They might be home, though."

"Thomas, are you going to let them bully you for the rest of your life? Are you planning on allowing them to steal all your possessions and sell them on eBay?" He takes a few steps forward. "This is not about fear or pride anymore. This is about Melissa."

"All right, you are right." Thomas cradles his head in his hands miserably. "But I still can't go, I can't see her lying there dead…"

"Is it open casket?" Jas asks Benjamin. Apparently, she deems Thomas too messed up to rationally answer.

Benjamin just shrugs. "Could be. Really all depends on how long she was in the water and if they could get the swelling down to a normal level."

Thomas groans in pain. "I can't go tomorrow. I just can't go. Just thinking about it makes me feel..."

He doesn't get to finish his sentence before he dashes to the bathroom and vomits up everything in his stomach. His legs have turned to jelly while a thin layer of sweat covers every inch of his flesh. Any movement sends his head spinning and a fresh dose of nausea forces him to vomit again. When he opens his eyes, Jas is kneeling beside him with a wet washcloth.

"It's okay, Tom." She wipes his mouth gently like his mother might have done. "This reaction is perfectly normal."

"Please don't make me go," he whimpers, yet it sounds like he's dying as the words scrape his raw throat.

"We are all going," his uncle says from the doorway. "Thomas, listen to me. I never went to Helen's funeral. I even tried to stop anyone from planning a funeral for her. Now I regret it. I regret it every single day of my life, and I am not going to let that happen to you."

Thomas realizes the truth behind his uncle's words. He lets himself get sick one more time with Jas continuing to clean his mouth. "All right," he relents. "I will go."

Jas hugs him tightly, which his stomach objects to. They embrace a moment longer before they pull apart. Jas is laughing in relief, and Thomas feels awful for leaving her so on edge.

Benjamin pulls the car keys from his coat pocket. "Well, Tom, if your stomach ain't too jumpy, we can head over there now."

Jas looks so hopeful that Thomas has no desire to put it off. He nods at his uncle. "There's no time like the present I suppose."

12

The sky has grown overcast. It is not unusual for Wisconsin to host cold Octobers, but Thomas detects the crisp bite of potential snow. It is as if even the earth is mourning for Melissa.

Benjamin clears out half the backseat for Jas, throwing random car parts and boxes into the yard. Thomas climbs in next to his uncle and together, the haphazard trio drives to his parents' house. Even though it is where he has lived for thirteen years, it feels like going to a couple of strangers. He silently prays that his parents won't be home.

When they turn onto his road, he can see both of their cars parked neatly in the driveway. His stomach clenches with nausea at the thought of facing them again. He feels like he is going to be sick for sure but fights against it. Like his uncle said, this is no longer about fear or pride. This is all about Melissa.

They park on the street and follow his uncle to the door. None of them want to ring the doorbell or knock, but they are saved by his mother opening it from the inside. This makes Thomas wonder if she has been watching for him to come home, and the thought brings him a little comfort.

That comfort dissipates with her next words. "What are you doing here?"

Benjamin answers gruffly. "We are going to Melissa Down's funeral tomorrow afternoon and Thomas needed to pick up some clothes for the occasion." Elise stares back blankly, and Thomas can hear the anger growing in his uncle's tone. "You know, that little girl who was raped and died? I know you are just so perfect, Elise, but maybe a scrap of humanity left in you can feel some empathy."

"Don't you dare speak like that to me after what you did to my sister."

"What? Do you think I hired that loser to rape her and then threw her off the bridge?" He is clenching and unclenching his hands by his sides. "Don't try twisting the story now, Elise, because the truth is, you never cared to hear it in the first place."

The two stare at each other for what feels like an eternity. A noise by the staircase causes Elise to break her stare. Allen strides over to stand protectively at his wife's side.

"What are you doing here, Ben?" he laughs bitterly. "You've got some nerve showing up here with my kid and some slut."

Heat rushes to Thomas's cheeks. "Jas is not a slut. How dare you call her that! She is a far better person than you'll ever be."

Allen looks like he's been slapped before realization turns into anger. Elise lays a hand gently on his arm to steady him. "Enough," she sighs heavily. "Why are you here, Thomas?"

Thomas feels like he has been punched in the gut. The blood evaporates from his veins and air seems to suffocate his lungs. This is his flesh and blood mother asking him why he, her thirteen-year-old son, has come home. He feels like a stranger—no, worse—like an intruder or some door-to-door salesman that you try to be polite with but secretly are annoyed by.

Yes, he chose to leave, but he never really thought he'd stay away forever. Some part of him had always imagined coming home one day to his mom's buttery cookies and her tender hugs. He didn't even mind his dad's negativity but had always tried to stay positive for his mom's sake. That was just the kind of son he was. Loyal to a fault and too obedient for his own good. It makes Thomas question whether he is just now discovering his true identity. Perhaps it is true that you have to lose everything before you can find yourself.

His uncle's voice brings him back out of his reverie. "Go grab your stuff, Thomas."

"Grab extra, Tom." his father adds. "I think it might be best to stay away for a while."

He is absolutely incredulous. His father just told him to stay away. Now he knows for sure that he is unwanted, but he reminds himself not to care. A family is not necessarily who you are born with, but rather who is there for you when times get tough. If all he has is his uncle Ben and Jas, then that is all he needs.

Wordlessly, Thomas squeezes past his parents into the house with Jas following him up the stairs to his room. Pulling a suitcase from beneath his bed, he layers his suit and other miscellaneous clothes into it, along with some dress shoes. It feels strange to finally have a need for the suit. His mom bought it for him around a year ago, saying he might as well have something on hand for special events in the future. While he wouldn't term Melissa's funeral as *special*, he certainly is relieved to be able to come dressed respectively.

He looks up when Jas starts laughing. "What is so funny?"

She gestures gleefully around the bedroom. "This room, all of it. I don't know why I am laughing I guess, but it is just such a relief to find someone like me."

"Which means what exactly?

"You're a geek! Come on, Stars Wars bedding? PlayStation 3 Skyrim edition?" She walks over and pulls a book off the shelf. "And of course your collection of Lord of the Rings is leatherbound."

"I like to be a geek with style," he says sarcastically.

"Looks like we have more in common than we thought."

Her comment lingers in the air like a pleasant fragrance while he continues to pack. He is conscious of the way she delicately picks items up to see them better before carefully setting them back down. It is as though every little detail catches her eye, and she can't ignore one of them. A strange emotion rises in his chest which he fiercely rebels against.

He lifts the suitcase onto the bed. "Ready to go?"

She holds up a twenty-sided dice for him to see better. He knows it well as it is his favorite, deep blue with yellow swirls like a hurricane. Instead of putting it down, she keeps rolling it around in her hand. "What is this for?"

"It's a twenty-sided dice." She rolls her eyes which makes him blush. "Um, but I use it to play Magic. Magic the Gathering is a really epic card game, but I'll spare you the details. Anyhow, you use those dice to keep track of your life. You start with twenty and slowly end up with nothing left, which is how you die."

"I feel like I'm at one health," she whispers.

"But that's what's cool about Magic," he offers. "You can always gain life back and try again. It isn't a game to just give up in. Heck, I've already won with one health left."

She smiles sadly, but it is tinged with hope this time. He walks over and folds her hand protectively around the little dice. "Keep it and don't forget to never lose hope."

Her eyes brim with tears that leak slowly down her cheeks. "Thank you." She hugs him tightly, and he feels her tears soaking the shoulder of his shirt.

They stay wrapped together for over a minute before Jas pulls away. No words are needed for the feelings being expressed at that moment. Together they walk back downstairs with a new resolve and more hope for the future awaiting them.

Thomas feels some of that hope fading when he finds his uncle arguing passionately with his parents again. Benjamin is gesturing angrily while Elise stands mute with her arms folded defensively across her chest. Allen doesn't seem too interested in the discussion but looks up to see Thomas and Jas walking down.

"Thank God you are done," he sighs in obvious relief. "It is best you all leave immediately. Just leave me and my wife in peace."

"Peace?" Benjamin nearly shouts. "What peace could you possibly find? A thirteen-year-old girl was raped and is dead, and all you can think about is getting your comfy lifestyle back. Well, it doesn't always work like that. It *shouldn't* work like that. Are you so blind that you cannot see how screwed up our world is becoming? We can't just sit back and do nothing!"

Thomas jumps at the sudden volume of his normally subdued mother. "So what are we supposed to do then? Hunt down every rapist on the planet, attend funerals, sit around and cry all day?" She raises an accusing finger shakily in Benjamin's direction. "I didn't even know this girl. She isn't my problem. Quit putting ideas in my son's head right now. You've corrupted him enough."

"I am not corrupting your son, I am supporting him!"

Now it is Thomas's turn to explode in rage. "Melissa is not a problem!" The scream tears through his throat like a knife, but the pain feels good. "Melissa was a young, sweet, innocent girl who had nothing wrong but was treated like trash up until her death. She is not the problem, rape is the problem, but you just ignore it like you do everything! If it inconveniences you even the slightest bit, you just turn a blind eye. Well, I am not going to do that anymore!"

"Suicide just isn't moral," his dad pipes up.

"Isn't moral? What is that supposed to mean?"

"Come on, Tom. She took her own life." He runs a hand through his greying hair, leaving it on the back of his neck. "It is a major sin to kill yourself. She could've been quite the inspiration, or maybe not let this rape rule her entire life."

"Do you think that there was literally any chance that a thirteen-year-old girl could live a normal life after something like that?"

Allen throws up his hands in defeat. "I would think so! Time heals all wounds and all that. She chose the easy way out and in my eyes, that makes her a coward."

Jas seems to be shrinking deeper and deeper into herself as if the words being thrown around are physically painful. Thomas can't just stop arguing, though, because to stop would mean giving up on Melissa, and that is something he simply cannot do. Not today, not tomorrow, not ever. She and every victim of the bridge is a part of him now.

"Things cannot stay the same anymore. Melissa did not choose the path of suicide, Asher did. There was nothing left for her, don't you see?" He realizes that his voice sounds like he is pleading, but he can't control it now. "Every victim, including Aunt Helen, was torn apart. Their identities were stripped away leaving them naked for the rapist to devour them. If no one does anything, then we are condoning that behavior."

He glances backward to see his uncle nodding proudly before meeting his father's eyes. "No one who sympathizes with a rapist is family of mine."

His parents try to call him back, and he feels his mother's hand catch on his wrist. He shakes her off and continues on his way to the car with his uncle and Jas trailing behind him. The second the doors close, they drive away; the tires desperately seeking traction. Thomas rolls down his window and breathes deeply. The cold air is biting, but right now he needs to feel something, anything, to know that he is still alive.

"How could he say that?"

Thomas twists around to see Jas curled up in a ball on the back seat. "My father doesn't think different is good. I know he believes what he said, and that's what I can't understand either. It doesn't seem possible to condemn a young girl like that."

She wipes a stray tear away. "That's what they did to Lisa, though."

"Who is Lisa? Was she your sister?"

Jas stares out the window for a few heartbeats, and Thomas thinks she isn't going to answer him. Then he sees her shoulders slump. "She was my twin sister. That's all I am going to say about it now."

"It might help to talk about it, Jas," he says gently.

"Just leave me alone, okay?" She sounds so defeated that he decides not to push things further.

The tension in the air is palpable. Thomas watches his uncle fumble in the glove box for a flask and then proceed to drink the unknown alcohol. He isn't sure why getting in a car accident scares him at all when living is just as frightening at the moment. The wind outside howling through the ill-fitted windows distracts him enough to retreat into his own thoughts.

13

They all file into Benjamin's house quietly. It feels like there is a force field around each of them, and any noise will set off an explosion. Thomas hates this feeling of detachment, but he doesn't quite know how to break it. He feels jumpy just sitting around, though, so he stands up to take laps around the living room.

Pictures cover the walls as if to hide the rosy wallpaper. He stops to inspect one of his aunt and uncle on their wedding day. Their faces are covered in cake and the photographer caught his aunt in mid-laugh. She is stunningly beautiful, and the look of adoration on his uncle's face proves how deep their love went. More than ever, Thomas wants revenge on the monster who stole the joy away from his aunt.

He carefully takes the frame off the wall and dusts it off on his sleeve. It feels sacrilegious to leave these memories covered in dust. There was so much happiness and laughter, futures to be fulfilled. Thomas feels an ache that he didn't try to get to know his aunt better. Why had he been so careless? Did it really take Melissa's death to make him see life in a new perspective? He was never one to believe in good coming from bad, but at least he can start to change things maybe.

Jas is nestled into a corner of the sofa, slightly buried in the sagging cushions. Thomas abandons his cleaning spree to go sit with her. She rests her head on his shoulder like a small child in need of comfort. "I wish none of this had ever happened," she sniffles. "I just want to feel happy again and have everyone back."

Thomas doesn't ask her what she means by "everyone" and just rubs her back soothingly. He shakes his head miserably. "Why did any of this have to happen? How did it even begin?"

"People suck, Tom. They always have and they always will. We try to define normal by what we think won't change or by whatever seems perfect. But you know what? I think that normal is just a figment of our imagination."

"So you don't think anything will ever be normal again?"

"When was anything ever normal to begin with?"

He ponders this as she cries into his shoulder. From the moment he was born he was considered *special* but never normal. The voices in his head make him question his own sanity on a daily basis. Still, he wants things to be normal again. Yes, the cookie cutter American life where young girls can still laugh and where families aren't divided. As much as he longs for this sense of security, though, he knows it can never be his. Nothing has a right to feel normal again.

"Hey, Jas?" She nods against him. "Should anything even have a right to be normal again?"

She sits upright. "What do you mean?"

"I mean, Melissa committed suicide, people get away with rape, and everyone turns a blind eye. Our society is as screwed up as it can get. Everything feels empty lately, and I don't know what I'm supposed to be doing anymore. I just don't see how normal can even be a possibility."

"You never really feel normal after it all," she says softly. "The hole in your heart just hurts a little less, but you never really wake up from the nightmare. All you can do is take one day at a time. I'm sure some people can find their own sense of normal after it all, but I would rather live in torture than forget."

They wrap their arms around each other, both of them weeping openly. It would seem awkward to an insider looking in, but to them it is all they can do to not fall apart. Thomas breaks away and smiles at Jas through his tears. "Thank you. It is nice to know I'm not alone."

She takes his hand in hers. "Just remember that they never really leave you. You'll never be alone as long as you keep their memories alive."

He realizes that his memories of Melissa are already fading. Little details about her are becoming foggy in his mind. "We need to write their stories down."

Jas jumps to her feet. "Let's start now. I need to be busy with something."

He smiles at her enthusiasm to work. "I feel the same way."

14

Benjamin walks into the room to find Thomas and Jas huddled over a notebook. "What are you guys working on now?"

"Thomas got the idea to write down the stories behind the victims of the bridge. Isn't it brilliant?"

"That's pretty smart, kid." He claps a hand firmly on his nephew's shoulder. "Sorry to be a downer, but we really need to start thinking about Melissa's funeral for tomorrow."

Thomas feels the familiar wave of nausea washing over him. He knows deep down why he hates the idea of going; because once the coffin is laid in the ground, everything becomes final. There will be no going back. It will mean that Melissa has completely slipped out of his grasp.

"I don't really have any funeral appropriate clothing," Jas mentions bashfully.

"You might fit into some of Helen's stuff. I'll find a few options for you to look through later on."

"Really?" She stares at him in awe, her mouth half open. "Won't that be disrespectful?"

"She would have liked having a young girl to pass her things on to."

Thomas barely hears the conversation as he slowly tears a sheet of notebook paper into shreds. He is conscious of his foot tapping irritatingly fast on the carpet, but nothing he does can harness his nerves. Jas seems to pick up on his tension and rests her foot over his own. "You doing all right there?"

He laughs awkwardly. "I don't remember what it feels like to be all right, so it's kind of hard to say yes or no."

She smiles sympathetically. "It'll get better. I know it doesn't seem like it will, but you just have to trust me."

"This is all for Melissa. If I mess this up, I'll never get another chance to make things right. I failed her once, I can't do it again."

"How did you fail her, Tom? How? Did you tell Asher to rape her? Did you twist her parents' minds to hate their own daughter?" Her voice rises in intensity and cracks as her throat thickens with unshed tears. "Thomas, think about the person who built that stupid bridge in the first place. You can spend hours trading blame back and forth, but all it'll do is eat you up inside and destroy the person you used to be."

Thomas takes a shaky breath and lets it out slowly. "You're right. I'm sorry, I just feel like I don't know what is up or what is down."

"If you didn't feel that way, I'd be worried."

His uncle clears his throat loudly. "If there's something I'm not thinking of that we need to do today, please feel free to let me know."

"A speech," Thomas says automatically. "Someone, and not her parents, needs to give a commemorative eulogy, something to preserve Melissa's legacy."

"Thomas, that isn't up to us." Benjamin leans forward to rest a hand on his nephew's knee. "We can't dictate how her funeral is run. But if you want, we can linger at the cemetery and pay our respects there."

He shrugs his uncle's hand off and stands up defensively. "If I don't *dictate* her funeral, then it's going to be trashed Her parents are just going to sugarcoat the whole thing to impress their fake friends. I won't let Melissa be treated like that! Even in death, she can't have peace? Why not? Why not, why not, why not, why not, wh..."

"Thomas, stop!" Jas is crying now, torrents of tears coursing down her cheeks. "You don't get to give a speech, ok? That isn't what Melissa would want. She'd want you to go, yes, but just act natural. Suicide victims usually don't want a lot of fuss. They want a quiet end, not speeches and music or whatever else people drum up for the funeral. If you want to respect Melissa, you'll pay your respects in quiet."

"Fine." All the fight drains out of him in that one word. "So...what? We are just going to go to the funeral then and sit quietly, then stay at the cemetery to pay respects in private?"

"I think that'd be best, Tom." Benjamin drags a hand tiredly over his eyes, a habit he is doing more and more often. "Jas, are you in agreement to what Thomas just said?"

She nods quietly as if she is afraid to disturb this moment of peace. They sit in silence for several minutes. It is less than twenty-four hours until Melissa's funeral, and it is sucking all of their energy. Benjamin is the first to move, rising from the sofa with a heavy groan.

"All right, kids. I'll show you where you guys are going to sleep."

Thomas and Jas follow him respectfully, even though they both know that neither of them is going to be able to sleep a wink. His uncle stops in the doorway of a small room with pale blue walls and blond wood floors. A twin bed is tucked into the corner with frilly white bedding on it. Despite the gauzy curtains and plush armchairs, the room has a cold aura to it. Thomas is reminded of a hospital room where you get sent before you die. A place for your visitors to come and say goodbye.

"This will be your room, Jas. The dresser has some of Helen's clothes in it, and the closet is empty except for shoes if you need to put anything in there. Otherwise, just make yourself at home."

She walks tentatively into the room like she is trying not to wake someone up. A handmade Raggedy Anne doll sits propped up on the bed and she picks it up, clutching it to her chest like a little girl. "Thank you," she whispers.

Benjamin starts walking to the next doorway, so Thomas feels compelled to follow. "This will be your room, Thomas. It isn't as cleaned up and pretty like Jas's room, but it was going to be your room if you had come to visit. Helen had always wanted to be closer, but your mom...she wasn't for the idea."

Thomas looks around the room, taking it all in. The walls are forest green, which makes the space feel small but still cozy. His feet leave dusty footprints in the dark grey carpet. A twin bed like Jas's is tucked beneath the window with a moose print comforter adorning it. Apparently, his aunt thought he was an outdoorsy kid.

"I love it." He means it too. Despite the fact that the decor is a complete opposite of his personality, he feels a connection to the room. He can imagine his aunt going to the store and thinking what her nephew might like. More than ever, he wishes that he had been given the chance to meet this gentle, kind woman.

"I'll leave you to unpacking then."

Thomas doesn't have anything to unpack really, so he just hangs up his suit and tucks his suitcase in the closet. His watch reads that it is 8:35 pm. He sits there until it reads 9:15, unable to find the motivation to get up and actually do something. His phone vibrates in his pocket. No one ever texts him, so he chooses to ignore it, but it keeps vibrating insistently.

Pulling the phone out, he sees that Jas somehow got his number and has texted him multiple times already. *Come to my room*, is the last text sent. He doesn't even question it and nearly runs to her adjacent bedroom.

"Is everything ok?" He feels out of breath with worry.

Jas is curled up in the comforter on her bed. She looks different somehow, younger and more vulnerable. For a minute, Thomas can't figure out what has changed, and then he realizes that she is wearing no makeup. She is absolutely beautiful, her skin porcelain white with her eyes like silver stars.

"Can you sleep?" She whispers.

"No," he says, walking closer to hear her. "All I can do is think of every possible thing that could go wrong tomorrow."

She smiles wanly. "You're so optimistic."

He laughs softly at her attempt at sarcasm. "I just keep feeling like there is something I am supposed to be doing, something I am missing."

"That empty hole is never going to go away completely. You are always going to be looking for something to do that will fill in the gaps, but it just doesn't work that way."

"That doesn't make me feel much better."

"I guess it just helps me to cope with reality. It is kind of morbid, but I like knowing that I'm not living in some fantasy world."

Thomas stands awkwardly at the foot of her bed, picking at a loose thread in a pillow. He doesn't want to ignore reality, but he also wouldn't hate to feel happy again. It feels like a losing battle of emotions where there is no clear outcome of good or bad. Just to feel something and not be numb would be something of a success right now.

"Would you..." she chews on her lower lip. "Would you sleep with me tonight?"

A thousand scenarios fill his mind. Sleeping with a girl is not something he would ever consider because that road just leads to sex. But then he looks at Jas, who is staring at him with a pleading look in her big grey eyes, and he realizes that she just needs someone to fight her demons with her.

Wordlessly, he pulls back the comforter as Jas wiggles closer to the wall to make room for them. They lay there silently, with the comforter heavy on them and her foot touching his own. It feels safe with someone close to him, and for once he doesn't feel quite so alone. They are both suffering, but the suffering has also bonded them closer together.

If his parents knew he was sleeping with a girl three years older than him, he would be grounded for life. But this isn't romantic or lustful. It feels like Jas is his older sister, and they are pulling together to get through this difficult time. If it wasn't for her, he doesn't know how he could hold himself together.

He rolls over slightly to face her and finds that she has miraculously fallen asleep already. All the worry lines are gone, and she looks innocently peaceful. As much as he wants to talk about tomorrow and sort through his feelings, he doesn't have the willpower to wake her up. Instead, he lies there quietly and goes through every memory he has of Melissa.

He remembers the first time that he saw her. It was the first day of school that year and everyone was being loud and rowdy because the teachers just don't care yet. But Melissa was just quietly reading at her desk, her raven black hair falling over her eyes. She was beautiful like a piece of glass. It seems as though anything could break her, but she was so gorgeous no one risked touching her.

Melissa never skipped school, and she would stay late studying at the library like she didn't want to go home. He always watched her from a distance but never had the courage to go up and talk to her. Now he regrets that more than anything. How could he have been so careless? Was he so scared of rejection, and if so, why? Suddenly his reverie is broken by a whimper coming from Jas. She is awake now and crying softly into her pillow.

"Hey, what's wrong?"

"Just a bad dream," she manages to choke out.

He props himself up on one elbow to look at her. "Do you want to talk about it?"

She starts to shake her head but then sighs. "It was about my twin sister. You might have already guessed, but she...she killed herself at the bridge."

"Hey, we don't have to do this now."

"So when should we discuss it? Tomorrow at the funeral? Next week?" She squeezes her eye shut to stem the tears. "There is no perfect time to talk about grief, Tom."

He rubs her shoulder gently like his mother had done for him. It has never been easy for him to commiserate with others, but he is slowly learning. Jas takes a shuddering breath which she releases slowly.

"So, we were both fourteen years old, obviously. I mean, we were twins and all. But we weren't the clingy twin sisters you'd see in movies. We never dressed the same, and she kept her red hair long while I cut mine short and bleached it." She pulls the comforter closer to her chin.

"What I regret most is how we would go out of our way to be separate. We never celebrated our birthdays together, never ordered the same flavor of ice cream, and most of all, we never ever went to school together. She would walk, and I would take the bus."

She is crying in earnest now, her chest rising and falling painfully. Thomas wants to tell her, beg her, to stop, but he realizes that she needs to let it all out. Like his uncle did with his Aunt Helen. Gradually, her sobbing quiets down so she can speak again.

"It was December 8th, but it hadn't snowed yet. I told her to take the bus because it was way too cold to walk outside, but she just ignored me as usual. So I just told her to do whatever she wants. Kill herself if that's her goal in life." Jas is gasping now, gulping for air like her lungs are constricted. "That...that was..."

"That's the last thing you said to your sister." Thomas is morbidly awestruck by the horror of it all. The weight of her guilt is like a presence in the room, haunting them with invisible terrors.

"I told her to kill herself. I told her to die!" She weeps continually, barely containing herself any longer. "She... she didn't seem bothered by my rudeness at the time. I remember her rolling her eyes and calling me a loser before trotting off to school. She was wearing her new leggings that day. Mom never let us wear leggings, but for Lisa's birthday, she bought her a black pair with little hearts all over them.

"That was the last I saw of her. We didn't do open casket, so I didn't get a chance to see her again even in death."

Thomas swallows uncomfortably. "What made her... you know..."

"Rape." Jas spits the word out like venom. "I don't know who, but that's what the notes said. *Sorry, Jas, you were right about taking the bus. I can't write it. I'm too scared, Jazzy, so, so, so, so, scared. He raped me. I can't live with that. I love you and mum so much.* That's what her note said."

"Where did she leave the note?"

"It was in her backpack still sitting on the bridge. She never came home from school so mum called the police. She always overreacts, but this time she actually was right. Oh, was mum hurt when the note was mainly addressed to me. But I guess under all the arguing, we still had that sisterly connection."

"I'm so sorry." It is the lamest comment on earth.

"Me too. I really loved her too. I just was a moody girl who didn't know how to express my emotions. For weeks afterward, if I left somewhere, I'd always tell mum I love her, and she'd just ask me why."

"That doesn't make sense."

"Or does it? Lisa's death broke us so deeply that my mum no longer believes in true love. So, me telling her that is like saying the house is on fire when you live underwater."

"That is the most bizarre analogy I have ever heard."

She smiles through her tears. "You are such a nerd, Thomas. I just told you my darkest secret and all you can do is comment on my killer analogy."

He blushes self-consciously. "Sorry, I'm not too good at emotional expression."

"Welcome to the club," she says drily.

"Thank you for telling me. It means a lot, and I know that must have been really hard to relive." He pauses for a heartbeat. "Don't blame yourself, Jas. Not for anything. Not for last words, or what could have been or should have been. You didn't want this to happen. I guarantee she knew you loved her, Jas. That note says it all."

Jas breaks down in loud, ugly sobs. A light comes to life in the hallway but goes dark a few seconds later. Thomas slides closer to Jas and wraps an arm hesitantly around her. She clings to him for dear life, her nails digging holes in his back. He feels wetness on his cheeks and realizes that he is also crying now.

All of their emotions pour out with neither of them fully conscious of the other. The pain in Thomas's heart feels like an open wound that keeps healing only to get torn apart over and over and over again. The black hole yawns wider, swallowing them into an oblivion of sorrow.

Their tears slowly dry as sleep overtakes them. They fall asleep in each other's arms, seeking any protection in the storm. Sleep is a welcome boon right now, for it offers an escape from the torture of what has become their reality.

15

Thomas wakes up in a fog. The comforter is white instead of his assigned moose print. His feeling of disorientation dissolves when he remembers last night and the confession Jas made. He vows to himself never to divulge her secret unless she permits it. He slowly raises himself away from the pillow, quietly edging out of the covers. She deserves to rest, and if sleep brings her any peace at all, then he hopes she chooses to sleep in late.

His bare feet pad rhythmically down the wooden hall to his room. Gently closing the door behind him, he ventures to turn on a light. Half blinded by the sudden brightness, he stumbles his way over to the closet where his suit hangs resentfully. Thomas feels grimy after over a day of sweating and not showering, but he just doesn't have the energy.

The suit hangs awkwardly on his narrow frame, confirming that everything about this day is absolutely wrong. A fresh wave of nausea washes over him as he thinks of Melissa lying on a metal table with her blood draining out her veins. As much as he longs to push the memory out of his mind, he holds onto it. He relishes the disturbance it causes him because he feels there can be no more peace or ignorance after her death.

He jumps at a soft knock on his door. It cracks open a bit to expose half of his uncle's face. Thomas stiffens in his suit, folding his arms over his chest tightly. "It doesn't fit."

"Tom, you and I both know it fits. Now I reckon you have probably never worn a suit before like this, and the first time is always a trial. Just pretend you're wearing jeans and a flannel, and the rest will follow."

Right, like anyone could pretend that they're dressed for a woods hike when in reality, they are attending a funeral. Is his uncle out of his mind? Thomas doesn't even bother to reply as he scrutinizes his appearance in the mirror.

"When I was your age, I went to my first funeral too."

This piques his interest just a bit. "Did you know who it was for?"

His laughs humorlessly. "Yeah, yeah I did. It was my dad's funeral."

The blood freezes in Thomas's veins. Everything he says lately is so cold, so unfeeling. All he can do is come up with the lame old standby. "I'm, um, I'm really sorry."

"Well, that's humans for you. We live like idiots, and then death comes around and no one is ready for it. They always say you've got your life ahead of you as a kid, you know? Look at Melissa! Her life ended far too prematurely." He shakes his head miserably. "You never know how many years you got, Tommy. Any of us could die today or twenty years from now. But death is inevitable. You can't ever forget that, Tommy. Death is our primary motivation. To see how we can make an impact, a name for ourselves, before death comes to take us home."

It isn't the inspirational speech of the year, but Thomas knows how his uncle thinks. This is like poetry for him. Hot tears prick the back of his eyelids as he swallows the hard lump forming in his throat. "You're right."

His uncle smiles faintly. "Of course I am." He throws a comb at Thomas who ends up dropping it. "Now comb that hair of yours and let's get moving."

He leaves Thomas alone with his thoughts, carefully closing the door like a loving father. Even a week ago, Thomas never would have expected to become so close to his Uncle Benjamin. He had lived all thirteen years of his life with no notion that the man existed. Now he was like a second father. A better father at the moment than his biological one in fact.

Thomas quickly runs the plastic comb through his hair, letting the natural buildup of oil keep it from frizzing up again. After one last glass in the mirror, he leaves the room. Knowing what is coming turns his legs to jelly as he wanders into the kitchen.

Jas is sitting at the table wearing a peach-colored dress and creamy heels. She wears a long-sleeve cardigan which hides her arms from view. Her hair looks damp, so she must have done what he hadn't and showered. She is once again wearing makeup, but it is lighter than when he first met her. Her eyes meet his and she blushes slightly.

"You look like a girl," he blurts out.

His uncle sprays coffee out of his mouth in a bark of laughter. "Well aren't you a regular philosopher! You realized she is a girl. Congratulations, buddy."

"He is a genius," Jas deadpans.

Thomas feels the heat rising up his neck and can imagine his face turning beet red. "Very funny, haha." He takes a seat at the little table where his uncle lays a plate of artificially yellow eggs down.

"After you finish eating, we'll head over to the funeral."

Jas stares at her food as if willing it to disappear, but Thomas knows that his uncle is trying his best. He forces himself to pick up some eggs, chew, swallow, and repeat until his plate is clear. Benjamin looks shocked by his sudden appetite but makes no comment. He glances at Jas's untouched plate.

"Not hungry this morning?"

"I'm a vegetarian." While Thomas does not doubt this, it seems too convenient of an excuse in the given moment.

His uncle jangles his keys between his hands. "Ready when you guys are."

They file out into the brisk October morning. It is getting close to the end of the month, and Thomas thanks his lucky stars that he is too old for trick-or-treating. There is no way he could glean enough enthusiasm to pull it off.

The little car sputters courageously but seems determined not to start. Benjamin curses under his breath as he attempts to start the car a third time. It sputters weakly to life, and Thomas feels his hopes drop. He didn't even know he had any hopes, but now he realizes that if the car wouldn't start, they wouldn't be able to go.

Jas is a ghost in the backseat; present but silent. His uncle is the complete opposite. "This weather is crazy, huh? All those kids are going to freeze this Halloween. Speaking of which, I should probably start thinking of getting some candy pretty soon, shouldn't I? What's y'all's favorite type of candy?"

"Jolly Ranchers." Thomas can't believe he can even think about candy at a time like this, but the response was so automatic he barely even had time to think about it. Benjamin remains silent as though waiting for something that never comes.

"Never could get around to fancying those myself," his voice is soaked in false cheeriness. "I like caramels, but Helen always had a thing for licorice whips. Like Twizzlers, you know? She'd separate the strands and eat them all one by one so delicately."

Helen's memory ends the conversation. All these people are no longer on earth, yet their memories loom larger than ever. They were too good, gone too soon. Thomas wants to say something meaningful, something to heal the wound they left behind, but instead, he turns to stare out the window.

16

The remainder of the drive passes in tangible silence like a heavy blanket. All of the spaces in the church lot are filled, so his uncle parks half a block away on a side street. Jas's heels tap merrily on the road as if excited to be of use again. With every step, Thomas feels his stomach tighten. He keeps his hands in his pockets to keep them from shaking, but his nerves run high.

A wave of pure rage washes over Thomas when he sees Melissa's parents greeting everyone at the church entrance. They shake hands pleasantly, thanking everyone for coming, asking them to make themselves comfortable. Don't they know that this isn't some dinner party? This is their only daughter's funeral and they are just blowing it off.

Thomas leads the way up the steps, his feet marching like he's headed off to war. Mrs. Downs dabs an invisible tear away from her perfectly mascaraed eyes while her husband reaches out a hand. Thomas regards it as a dead fish and keeps his own hands firmly in his pockets. Benjamin and Jas follow his lead, all walking stoically into the church without a backward glance.

The crowd takes the air from his lungs. There must be over a hundred people, and not everyone has even arrived. He wonders how many of these guests actually knew Melissa, or if they are merely attendants of the Downs' outrageous parties.

They take a seat near the back. By the altar is a mahogany pedestal with a golden urn resting atop it. His limbs go numb. Melissa must have been too deformed for an open casket, so for appearance sake, her parents opted for cremation. All that is left of his darling is black dust.

Jas covers his hand with her own while looking straight ahead. Her eyes are glassy, but she makes no move to clear away the tears. Suddenly it dawns on him that his own eyes remain dry as a desert. Why is he not sobbing, breaking to pieces? Where is his humanity? Is this not the funeral for the girl he loved?

Even the phonies are showing the appropriate emotions. He looks at his uncle's pale green shirt and Jas's peachy dress. They look like a family out for Easter Sunday. Rather than sadness, all he feels is anger. He is mad at his parents for not coming, mad at the Downs for their petty lives, and he is furious with himself for not crying. It is as though the world has been flipped upside down, and he is drowning underwater.

An elderly man, whom Thomas assumes is the pastor, walks to the front of the church. He wears a somber expression drenched in sympathy. There is a gleaming white bible in his wrinkled hands, which he opens to read John 14:27 aloud.

"Peace I leave with you; my peace I give you. I do not give to you as the world gives. Do not let your hearts be troubled and do not be afraid." He smiles faintly at the audience. "Melissa was a lovely young girl, full of life and kindness. We are dearly sorry for the loss of her life but know that she is safe and at peace with her father in Heaven."

Was she Christian, though? Thomas never felt that she was. Still, the verse offers him some comfort. Then her parents are called to the stage where Mrs. Downs clutches a tissue and gives her husband the mic.

"Thank you all for coming here today. This is a tragic and difficult time, but as always, our friends have only drawn us closer. Her life was so short. Let it remind us all to live life to the fullest every day, and free ourselves from any future regrets. Thank you."

Thomas looks at Benjamin whose jaw is practically on the floor. He jabs Thomas in the ribs. "Can you believe it? He never once mentioned love or *daughter*. He never even shed a tear!"

He keeps staring straight ahead. Yes, he agrees with his uncle, but he can't let his emotions loose yet. There is too much at stake and, unlike her father, he will not be letting Melissa down ever again.

Others rise from the crowd to give eulogies, but they praise Melissa's parents more than she herself. Benjamin yawns loudly, then looks sheepish at his disrespect. Thomas cannot help but shoot him a dirty look. His gaze travels past his uncle, however, to a man standing near the exit in jeans and a casual polo. He is scribbling furiously in a notebook like a journalist would be doing at a red carpet event. Yet despite the seriousness of the occasion, this man is smiling like a Cheshire cat.

Renewed fury courses through Thomas's veins. He kicks Jas's ankle to which she sends him an equally hard jab in the knee. He cocks his head in the man's direction, and her expression changes from irritated to curious.

"Who is that?" she mouths exaggeratingly.

Thomas shrugs while fixing his eyes on the stranger. The man looks at his watch startled, then hastily begins stuffing the notebook in his bag.

"If my uncle asks where I am, I went looking for a restroom."

"Tom, what are you..."

Her whisper fades to nothing as Thomas follows the man away from the funeral. He cannot believe he is really doing this, walking out on his beloved Melissa. But this could be someone who works for the paper, someone who knows the writer for the obituaries.

The man is walking fast and soon exits the church. Thomas follows him at a safe distance while pretending to be fascinated by his phone. In reality, he is texting himself details of the man such as height, dress, behavior. Turning a corner onto Maple Lane, the man gets into a shiny black Nissan. He frantically adds the license plate number to his list of suspect details before heading back into the church.

He walks slowly, trying to calm his breathing to a semi-normal pace. An exodus of guests is exiting the church. Jostled to the front are Jas and Benjamin, scanning the sea of people expectantly. Thomas jogs over to them breathlessly.

"I'll explain on the drive."

His uncle looks extremely cross. The funeral must have brought back too many painful memories and his nephew's disappearing act was the last straw. He turns in the driver seat to face Thomas. "It's about eight minutes to the cemetery, so get talking."

"Okay, okay…" He takes a deep breath. ", I was kind of freaking out in there. Then you did the mega yawn, and when I looked at you, I saw a man taking notes. He was dressed too casually to be a part of the funeral, and he was *smiling*.

"Anyhow, he was writing so frantically that I figured it must be important. He kept looking up at the people giving eulogies, but his smile never once faded. He looked like a journalist. So I followed him to see where'd he go next."

He uncle relaxes his tight grip on the wheel. "What did you find out?"

"Not much. I texted myself some details about the guy himself, but otherwise, all I found out was the model and plate number of his car."

"That isn't a bad start kid. Sorry for getting so angry about it."

"Nah, that's all right. I went about it stupidly, so it isn't anyone's fault."

Benjamin nods philosophically. "You've got some sound judgment there, kid."

The last few minutes are passed in silence. Despite this enormous breakthrough, Jas hasn't made a sound or even shown that she's been listening. He understands that what she went through with her sister was tough, but this pity party she keeps throwing isn't helping anyone.

They keep to the back of the crowd at the cemetery. A light rain has begun to fall, which dampens the mood even further. Everyone raises their umbrellas to form a solid black ceiling. Thomas stands with his makeshift family in the rain, feeling claustrophobic with so much black. The pastor says a few more words of false reassurance for

Melissa's soul before the ashes are lowered into the musky earth. People throw roses and lilies into the grave before the dirt gets shoveled back into the hole. Thomas looks away, feeling sick, but no closer to crying than he was before.

They wait silently for the funeral party to leave before walking up to the headstone. Jas traces the engraved letters delicately with her finger, tears streaming down her face. "She was so young."

Thomas sniffs disdainfully. "No kidding. Asher sure is lucky he didn't come."

"What would you have done, Thomas?" Jas asks tiredly. "Obviously, someone like Asher would never show up to a funeral. That would be too honorable. But your busted lip says you'd be creamed by him."

He looks at her with hardened eyes. How dare she be so judging, so indifferent. "At least I'd try instead of just letting Melissa suffer alone. I don't abandon people, Jas."

She recognizes the connection between the insult and her sister. Her lower lip trembles pitifully, and Thomas immediately wishes he could snatch his last words back. "Maybe you could take him on, Thomas. You two may have more in common than you think."

His uncle watches their exchange in confusion but says nothing. Either he is just too tired or he has given up on everything. Thomas cannot believe how fast everything spiraled in chaos in such a short amount of time. As much as he wants to apologize to Jas for his behavior, the words lodge themselves in his throat.

They head back to the car with the weight of the unknown pressing heavier upon them. Melissa's life may be over, but the race to avenge her death is only beginning.

17

Thomas cannot imagine sitting through visitation. All it would be is a stuffy room filled with uncaring zombies. Everyone will be clutching crinkly, dry tissues to swipe at nonexistent tears. Thus, they skip visiting to drive straight to the library. Jas has finally come back to life, leading them at a quick pace. His uncle directs them to the "off limits" section by periodicals where they each take a seat next to a monitor.

"Calm down, Tom." Benjamin gives him a knowing stare, and only then does Thomas realize that he's been drumming his fingers as the fossilized computer revives itself.

"Oh, sorry," he mumbles under his breath. Jas's computer is the first to load as she jabs the keyboard viciously. Clearly, she is not over their fight.

"Hey..." he stumbles around for the right thing to say. "You were right about me having an ugly attitude back there."

"Uh, yeah, I know that." Her grey eyes, though burning with anger, are brimming with tears. She takes a shaky breath and releases it slowly. "Some people just never change."

Her words cut him deep, but he knows that he deserves it. After all, he just insulted her using her twin sister's suicide. How could he, after she told him the darkest most painful part of her life?

"Hey Ben, look at this."

Even though Thomas was clearly excluded from the viewing, he scoots next to Benjamin to peer at the smudged screen over Jas's shoulder. Three pictures of middle-aged to aging men smile back with perfectly white, straight teeth and slicked back hair. These are the primary journalists for the local paper in Clermont.

His uncle points to a man with salt and pepper hair cropped short. "That is Davis Larks, he is retiring next month. A pity, too, because he is the only one with any talent."

They all turn their focus to the other two remaining journalists. The aging man is Markus Jacobson, while the dirty blond man who appears much younger is Liam Knotham.

"That guy, what is his name....Liam? Yes, Liam was at the funeral, I guarantee it." Thomas is savagely tapping the screen with his finger, adding to the collection of smudges.

Jas rolls her eyes exaggeratingly and sighs. "You were even more high strung than usual. I doubt you would have recognized your own family in the state you were in."

Her grey eyes spark with a challenge to contradict her. He has so many little jabs that he could make right now, and the temptation is difficult to resist. But he already hurt her once, so he chooses to surprise her. "Yeah, you're right. I wasn't myself. Let's check them both out better."

The look of shock on her face is priceless, but Thomas refuses to let himself revel in it. She modulates her voice to hide the sudden surprise. "Absolutely. Hey, Ben, could we maybe print out their bios?"

He holds up several sheets of paper. "Done and done."

Thomas looks at his watch. "It is five o'clock; the library will be closing in half an hour."

His uncle looks at each of their ragged faces. "What about getting some dinner out first?"

Thomas is touched by the offer. He knows that his uncle is not rich, and splurging on a meal out for all of them is no small fare. Neither he nor Jas says yes or no but merely stand up to graciously accept his offer.

Once in the car, he asks them where they'd like to go. Thomas remains silent, willing Jas to open her mouth and say something, *anything*, and give her own opinion. Finally, he receives the one-word answer. "Chinese."

His uncle seems pleased. "Chinese it is then."

This feels like a deliberate blow to Thomas. He despises Chinese food with a passion, but he bites his tongue and forces an unnatural smile onto his face. The restaurant is extremely crowded for a Saturday night, so they wait on satin chairs stained by grease, sweat, and the unknown. Tinkly music plays in the background with unintelligible words mumbled in their native language. Everywhere he looks he sees pandas staring back at him clutching bamboo. The whole thing is making him very claustrophobic and he really wishes they would be led off to their table soon.

"Table for three?" The waiter seems to appear out of thin air.

"Yes, thank you." His uncle is all courtesy.

They sit at a table near a fountain which must be meant to be soothing, but Thomas really just wants to unplug it. A koi fish winks up at him, its mouth sucking open and closed like it is gasping for air that doesn't exist. He wonders if that is what it feels like to be a fish, to constantly feel like you are drowning.

A menu plops down in front of him, breaking the reverie. Jas orders her food neatly, pronouncing the names carefully, while he and his uncle fumble to pronounce their choices. He barely glanced at what his choice entails, hoping it isn't too spicy.

They sit in uncomfortable silence for several minutes, absorbing the ceaseless laughter coming from nearby tables. Their food comes surprisingly fast, which Thomas finds strangely unnerving. He breathes a sigh of relief when his dish turns out to be rice with vegetables and long strips of beef. The first bite offers no overwhelming heat, so he is satisfied enough.

His uncle drags a chopstick around his plate but seems to be eating little to nothing. Then a glance over at Jas shows her using chopsticks expertly, even picking up the elusive bits of rice. She smirks triumphantly as Thomas fumbles to use even a simple fork, and he feels heat creeping up his neck.

"All right you guys, what's going on?"

Jas and Thomas both jump at the sudden sound of Ben's voice. Jas remains thoroughly fixated with her chopsticks, leaving Thomas to clean up the mess. "It's all my fault." He raises a hand to silence his uncle. "Don't even try to say that it isn't, because I guarantee you it is.

"We had all been leaving the funeral, and I said some really unkind things to Jas over practically nothing. I'd love to make excuses and say that it was because of my nerves, or the large crowd or whatever, but it was truly just me being stupid. I haven't been very thoughtful lately, and I know that I need to stop focusing on myself so much."

Jas looks up at him through half-open eyes. He sighs regretfully. "I am really, really sorry that I hurt you, Jas. I never meant to say those things, and I hope that someday I can make it up to you."

"I forgive you," she whispers.

He looks at her in surprise. "Really? You do?"

She laughs lightly. "It isn't helping any of us to hold a grudge so...yeah, I forgive you, Thomas."

He releases a sigh of relief. "Thank you, Jas. You are certainly the better person here."

"I know," she says with a mischievous smile.

His uncle seems much more relaxed now and proceeds to finish eating. They wait for what feels like hours to receive the bill before they finally head home. On the drive back, Thomas thinks about the all the mistakes he has made, and the regrets he lugs around with him every day. If he could go back and change things, he would. But at the end of the day, no one can go back in time and fix their past transgressions. All we can do is make the future a little brighter to outweigh the past.

Benjamin cuts the lights on the car and fumbles in his pocket for the house key. Once in the living room, he turns around slowly, critically analyzing the room. Jas and

Thomas share a confused look at this new behavior but say nothing.

"Helen never would have wanted to see her home treated like this."

Thomas waits for him to say something more. "Like... what do you mean?"

"Like this," he gestures empathically around the small room. "It is messy, abused, and neglected. I can't keep this up. Helen would not have wanted me to waste my life when her life ended so early. I'm going to change."

He disappears into the kitchen for a few moments and returns with a bucket of soapy water, a sponge, dusters, and a variety of cleaners. "Would you guys, um, mind helping me out a bit?"

Jas reaches out for a dusting cloth and a bottle of cleaner. "We would be happy to."

The three of them work for hours in the living room until it is sparkling clean. His uncle even throws the dirt-encrusted curtains in the washer. They all want to collapse on the furniture, but it seems too clean now to sully with their dirty clothes.

Benjamin wipes a smear of dust on his sweaty forehead. "You guys did a fantastic job. Thank you for helping. Now let's all shower and get some sleep, okay?"

Jas stumbles off to shower first, so Thomas helps his uncle put away the cleaning supplies. "That was very nice of you to apologize to Jas, Tommy. I know it can be hard sometimes, especially when it feels like you did nothing wrong. After Helen died...well, I said and did many things I don't even remember doing, but I am certainly reminded of it often."

Thomas nods solemnly. He doesn't want to be praised for apologizing to Jas. After all, if he hadn't said those harsh words in the first place, none of this would have been necessary. True, they are all on good terms now, but will she ever fully forget what he said? How much did it scar her soul, and can a scar ever be erased?

Jas calls from her room that the shower is open, so Thomas heads in next. The water feels good after the past few days of grime covering his flesh. He takes longer than usual but then feels guilty when he realizes there might not be any hot water left over for his uncle. Grabbing several towels, he hurries back to his room to get some needed rest.

Yet as he lies beneath the comforter that his aunt picked out, sleep evades him. He tosses and turns for hours, wrapping himself in the sheets tightly for security. Finally, exhaustion overwhelms him, and he drifts off to a restless sleep. Then his greatest fear that he has been harboring comes true. He dreams that he is with Melissa, and she is dying.

18

Thomas always knew that he would end up dreaming about Melissa, particularly her death. It is only natural, a part of the grieving process, but it still hits him like a bullet. He dreams that he is standing beside her on the bridge, dressed in his funeral suit. She is standing on her tiptoes, her feet bare and a white dress whipping around her thin legs from the wind.

"Don't jump," he pleads, his dream-self sobbing uncontrollably. "I need you, Melissa. I need you, and I always will need you."

She turns to face him, and it is painful to see her looking so alive. A strand of black hair blows into her eyes, and she pushes it back behind an ear. "No, you don't, Thomas. No one needs me. When I was alive, I was already dead."

"Please, don't do this, please, Melissa…"

She places one foot on the lower board of the railing and starts to climb. His heartbeat races in panic as the scene he has been dreading unfolds. Impulsively, Thomas reaches out to grab her arm, but it is like he grabbed thin air. He watches in slow motion as her tiny body falls from the railing to hit the water with a deafening sound.

Thomas wakes up sobbing, his skin covered in a layer of sweat. His chest aches like he himself hit the water, and his arm is red from where he must have been clutching at it in his sleep. He wants to talk about it and find comfort, but it is too personal to share yet. Slowly, his sobbing subsides. When will this torment ever end?

Suddenly the voices in his head return in full volume. He thought he was over this, but now it is like a crushing vice has been wrapped around his head as he cradles his skull in pain. It is impossible to discern what the voices are saying, but the noise alone is terrifying. "It is all in my head, all in my head..." He keeps up the mantra until finally, the noise subsides once more into merciful silence.

Thomas stumbles out of bed, pulling on some clean clothes he brought from home. After running a comb through his hair, he calls it good and wanders down to the kitchen. Benjamin and Jas are already pouring over a pile of old newspapers. Before they left the library yesterday, a librarian had given them some to keep, promising that no one would miss a few papers. By the tower on the kitchen table, Thomas would guess it is a lot more than just a few.

His uncle looks up at the sound of Thomas's footsteps. "Hey, Tommy, would you like some coffee?

Thomas hates coffee, thinking it tastes like stomach bile, but he needs to wake up and feel something. "Sure, that sounds good."

113

Benjamin rises with a grunt and goes over to the cabinet for a mug. He fills it half full with the rich, dark liquid before doctoring it up with whipping cream, sugar, and cinnamon sticks. "There you go, try that."

He takes a tentative sip and is shocked by how delicious it is. "This is amazing and...it doesn't taste like garbage."

Ben laughs heartily, and the sound of it lightens the mood tremendously. "Looks like we have another thing in common. I hate coffee, too, so I've learned how to make it tolerable."

Jas just shakes her head. "Black coffee is the only way to drink it, you babies."

"Maybe if you like tar!"

They all continue to chuckle lightly, and Thomas almost forgets his dream. Almost. It is like a festering disease in the back of his mind that will never fully heal. The wound scabs over, but he pulls it off to bleed anew.

He sighs. "So what are you overachievers up to this morning?"

Jas bounces on her seat like a child. "We decided to find out what this Liam dude writes about. I mean, he may be a suspect now, but what if he's writing the funnies?"

"So what have you found so far?"

"Well," Jas starts smugly. "I was up an hour before you and joined your uncle in the kitchen, which is when we started looking through these old papers. Apparently, Markus Jacobson only writes for the political columns. So he has been ruled out."

Benjamin looks so excited that Thomas knows good news is coming. Jas yawns and sifts indifferently through a stack of comics. "Well?" Thomas whines. "What about Knotham?"

She looks at him through half-hooded eyes. "Liam wasn't a full-time writer. He only wrote for the paper when he was needed to pen the obituaries."

Thomas grabs the nearest pile marked by a sticky note that has *obituaries* scrawled on top. Even just by scanning the words, he can clearly see the same sarcastic nature that was expressed in the unprinted obituaries from the suicides. He allows himself a small smile. "We have a target."

Benjamin claps a hand affectionately on his shoulder. "Tommy, I am just as elated as you are by the news. But remember, we cannot condemn this man immediately. He may yet be innocent."

Thomas shrugs. "He didn't publish the suicide victims' obituaries. I'd say that makes him guilty right there."

Jas is already nodding her head. "I agree with Thomas. This guy is just downright suspicious."

"But we can't just lower the guillotine on him! What if he lost someone to the bridge, and it is too painful for him to publish these things?"

"That doesn't make any sense," Thomas retorts. "If *you* had been the writer, would you have ignored Helen's death? No, and likewise I would have respected Melissa enough to give you a proper obituary. This man is an animal!"

"Enough!" Jas yells, raising her hands in a defensive gesture. "Just stop, will you? Arguing will only set us back. The only thing that can help us now is to get more information on Liam and decide if this is a lead worth following. Agreed?"

They mumble their agreements. Thomas just can't obey it, though. How can he, when he is so close to finding the murderer of his beloved Melissa? If he lets this go now, he may never have another chance.

"No." The force of that single word surprises even himself. He clears his throat. "We have to move faster. If he knows we are on to him, we may lose this lead altogether. I am done with moving slowly, being careful, or obeying every command. Together or alone, I am going after Liam. We have to pursue this."

His uncle's mouth is hanging open in shock. Jas just stares at him for several heartbeats before relenting to his speech. "I suppose you are right. It's all or nothing. I'm down."

"Count me in, too, Tommy. You are one amazing orator, ya know that?"

Thomas laughs harder than he has in days, maybe even his entire life. It isn't laughter from humor; there is absolutely nothing funny about their situation. No, his laugh comes from relief. All of the pain of losing Melissa has been bottling itself up in his soul, and he is finally learning to let it out.

Soon, Jas is laughing along with Thomas, and his uncle joins in heartily as well. They have needed this so much. For so long they have been just making it up as they go along, but now they have something real. There is no longer an invisible path but rather something tangible just within their grasp; if only they will have the courage to reach out and take it. Benjamin is the first to regain his composure. "How do we prove it is him?"

"We need more information," Jas decides. "If I can get ahold of his files, his background, then we might find another piece to the puzzle."

Thomas raises an eyebrow at his uncle, who rolls his eyes in return. "Let me guess. I'm supposed to hack the guy?"

"It is for a grand cause."

"All right, I'll do it. But after this, I am retiring my hacking skills."

Jas just shakes her head. "Such talent left unused…"

Thomas smiles at the friendly banter. Why can't there be more moments like this? This atmosphere is free of tension. His heart beats calmly, and the voices disappear. Then his blood turns cold. The voices…how could he forget them? Just a while ago he had woken up to the voices screaming in his mind. He wants to talk about it, to *scream* about it. Not yet, though. It is too fragile yet.

Jas breaks him out of their reverie. "All right, boys, get to hacking. I'm going to start searching in the papers one more time. Then we meet back here."

"Coffee makes you bossy," Thomas complains.

She smiles mischievously. "In that case, I'll just go make another cup."

While she scoops mountains of coffee grounds out of the tin, Thomas follows his uncle into the study where a dusty monitor sits in a corner. "This is for Melissa and Helen, Thomas. We won't ever give up."

He nods, but the lump in his throat prevents him from talking. They can never give up, and they never will.

19

J as feels a sense of peace in being alone in the kitchen. It isn't the same as being alone in her bed just sitting in the dark. Sleep always evades her, and she can sense her demons creeping closer, threatening to drag her under. She keeps waiting for the pain to ease. It has been two years since Lisa's death, but it still feels so potent.

Then again, why should the pain have to cease, or even soften? It is at least some sort of feeling, rather than just this perpetual numbness. A tear leaks out and dances down her cheek. Lisa was quite literally her second half. To have her gone is as physical a pain as losing a limb.

She drags her hand furiously across her cheek. For all her emo appearance, she really just wants to be loved. It is all a facade. She remembers when she was the girl with honey red hair braided down her back and horses on her shirts. Those were days of a carefree childhood. Now it is all replaced by darkness. Lisa took all of the light with her when she died.

More than ever, Jas wants to find this rapist and make him pay. In her mind, even the death penalty sounds too mild, but she'd never admitted that aloud. She feels less human for wanting to see this man tortured, and yet, that is exactly what makes her human. She wants revenge for her sister no matter what the cost may be. Fourteen years old is far too young for such harsh mutilation.

She shakes herself out of her reverie, downing another cup of black coffee. Unlike what she told Benjamin and Thomas, she despises black coffee. The thought of cream and sugar makes her mouth water, yet she won't allow herself even that little pleasure. Lisa always took her coffee black, and Jas will do the same. It is silly, petty even. But it lets her hold on to one more piece of her twin when all the other pieces seem to be fading away.

An old coffee cup covered in daisies sits on the table stuffed with pens, pencils, and highlighters. Jas selects a neon green sharpie to highlight any sections of the papers written by Liam Knotham. She realizes her suspicions are confirmed when she discovers that none of the printed obituaries are of the suicides. Does this mean that there is a connection perhaps? Her hand shakes from the anger building inside of her. Who does this man think he is?

A pattern slowly reveals itself as she watches his sarcasm and bitterness grow. Every obituary becomes even less compassionate and colder somehow. It is as though he is blaming these people for dying. How dare they allow a heart attack or cancer to take their lives. A wave of nausea hits her, whether from the heavy intake of caffeine or nerves she is unsure. Just then Thomas and Ben walk through the door, so she forces on an artificial smile. "Well, you're done early. Find anything helpful?"

Benjamin shakes his head angrily. "We would have, but the computer malfunctioned from some virus. I haven't renewed the security system since Helen died. It didn't matter at the time, but now I wish I had. We are losing precious time."

Thomas nods. "The computer is running a sweep now, but it could take hours."

Jas feels her stomach drop. She had been hoping to discover some brand new lead, something convicting to send this man to his doom. She tries to chide herself for such morbid thoughts, but it is hopeless. She wants to see this man suffer, no matter the cost. "A few hours?" she echoes.

Benjamin sighs regretfully. "Maybe more...I don't know." He eyes the mass of papers littering the table. "Do you need some help?"

She hesitates. This feels like her personal mission, but it would be more practical to have two extra sets of eyes scanning the pages. "Sure. I've been highlighting anything written by Knotham. So far, it has all just been obituaries, and his attitude only worsens as the dates become more recent." Jas notices a spark of hatred flash in Thomas's eyes. Then something like pain crosses his face. "Tom, are you all right?"

Benjamin looks over at his nephew, and his face contorts into concern. "Tommy, what's the matter? Does your head hurt?"

"Some...something like that."

Benjamin eyes him more carefully. "Let's go talk in private, Tommy."

Thomas follows his uncle out into the living room like a loyal puppy. Jas is frustrated at having been left behind, but she understands that whatever this is, it must be very serious. Her concern overtakes her annoyance, and she finds herself unable to work on the papers.

20

Thomas is frustrated with himself over being a psychopath. Why can't he just be normal? How is he ever going to explain this to his uncle? But this is his family now. If he keeps this secret tucked away inside of him, he can never fully save Melissa's legacy. After all, how do you save someone else when you can't even save yourself?

"So, what has been going on, Tommy?"

He scuffs his toe into the carpet. "You will think I've lost my mind."

"No I won't," he says gently. "Come on, Tommy, something is seriously bothering you. I can tell, and so can Jas."

Thomas hates himself for wearing his emotions so openly on his sleeve. Other people can hide their feelings so well, just tuck them away, but not him. He cannot hide anymore, though.

"It is these voices. I don't exactly know how to explain it even. They just suddenly start screaming in my ears, in my mind actually." He starts speaking more rapidly, all of it pouring out of him at last. "It used to be just whispers, but now it is so much more. I don't know what to do."

"Like voices of the dead?"

Thomas looks up quickly. "How did you know that?"

"Because the same thing happened to me. After Helen died I was lost. Then the voices came, and I welcomed them in. Anything to dull the ache of abandonment. But then I realized I was allowing demons to replace my Helen, so I fought back."

"When did you stop hearing them?"

"About two months ago." He sees Thomas's face fall discouragingly. "Things take time to heal, Tom."

"I guess Melissa's death made it worse but...I have been hearing these voices my whole life."

His uncle is taken aback by this new revelation. "I will admit that is a more severe case then, but the same rule applies. Fight back, Tommy. Don't ever give up."

It seems like all of the advice lately is about not giving up, yet that is exactly what he wants to do. Instead of whining like a little kid, though, he forces a smile and thanks his uncle.

"Anytime, Tommy. Now let's go back in there and help Jas out, okay?"

Jas is staring at them when they walk in. Clearly, she was not working and rather was listening to their subdued conversation. The thought annoys Thomas, but he brushes it aside. After all, he has gotten in enough fights with Jas recently, and the world has enough strife in it without petty disagreements.

"Hand Thomas and me a highlighter, would you, Jas?"

She wordlessly hands them each a highlighter, giving Thomas a bright pink one. Again he bites his tongue. Why is she so upset about him having a private conversation with his uncle? She isn't even family. He presses the highlighter into the page like he can burn a hole through all of his problems. Jas notices and gives a huff of exasperation. "Geez, Thomas. You are blurring all of the words. You're no help at all!"

It is the last straw. Thomas rolls up the page and throws it in her face. "I never wanted to help! But I did, and now it has to be your way again. Always whatever Jas wants, huh?"

"You two again." He uncle caps his own highlighter to assess them. "Why are you always fighting? I thought we were a team."

"Well, she was listening to our conversa..."

"He just can't calm down ever..."

"Enough!"

They both sit down sheepishly and stare at their hands. Whenever Benjamin raises his voice, people tend to cower. It holds an ominous threat of the wrath behind his tone, and that is something no one wants to tangle with. "Look," he says more softly. "We are all stressed and we haven't had any real break from all this. But we can't chew each other apart either. We are barely surviving as is. If we break apart, what will we have left?"

Thomas feels ashamed of himself. His uncle has lost so much already, and now he has to put up with their trivial fighting. He glances up at Jas and sees a similar expression mirrored on her face.

"I'm sorry, Thomas."

"Me too, Jas. I know I've been snapping at you a lot, and I really will try to stop."

She nods slowly. "So will I. It takes two to tango, as the saying goes."

Benjamin sighs in relief. "See? It is a lot easier to get along when we aren't arguing. Five more pages each and then we call it quits for now, okay?"

Thomas agrees but Jas is more reluctant. It is obvious that this means a lot to her, but even she can see that a break will do more good than harm. Suddenly, she speaks up after several minutes of silence.

"This is rather depressing, isn't it?"

Thomas can't remember a time when he wasn't depressed but is still confused by what she means exactly. "What is depressing?"

"All of this," she gestures largely at the mass of papers strewn across the tabletop. "So many deaths have been mutilated by this man who can't write a respectful obituary to save his life." She blushes at her choice of words on the topic of death.

"You're right, though." She brightens at Thomas's positive attitude. "I mean, even if they *were* written properly, it is still such a staggering amount of death. Sometimes it feels like nothing else exists."

"So don't let them die for nothing."

They look at Benjamin in surprise, at his philosophical change of attitude. He looks like he wants to melt into the floor, but instead, squares his shoulders defiantly. "I mean, think about it. We mourn for those who have died, but they are at peace. Helen, Melissa, and those others whom we don't know, they are all at rest now. It is left to us to decide whether or not they disappear forever. We have to keep their memories alive, preserve their legacies, and never forget."

Thomas feels moved by the speech. "But how can we do that? We are just...us."

"You are never just *you*, Tommy, and we are never just *us*. One spark starts a wildfire, so three of us can make an inferno. It might be painful, but we really cannot forget them. We have to talk about them in the present."

Jas is playing with a highlighter, deep in thought. "So we have to share memories of them, don't we?"

"Don't sound so sad, Jas, it can even be fun. My Helen meant the world to me, and it hurts so much to even say her name. But I love her too much to let her go. I can't, and I won't."

"I think it's a great idea, Uncle Benjamin."

"There is something I told Thomas but not you," Jas stares at Ben. "Could I share first?"

He looks apprehensive at first. "Sure, Jas, go on."

She stares at her hands. The skin around her nails is red and fraying like she chews them often. "My twin sister, Lisa, was fourteen years old when she was raped. I...I said some awful things to her before she left for school one day, and then she just...just never came back." She squeezes her eyes shut to quench the tears that threaten to spill. "I...I can't even remember the bad times. They are fuzzier, like a photograph that is out of focus. The good memories, though, those are clear and vibrant. Sometimes I think I will see her walking around town, and then I have to go to the bridge and remind myself that she is really truly gone. Gone forever."

Ben places a hand tenderly on her arm. "They never really leave. Maybe you did say some mean things, and I won't pry, but I guarantee that Lisa knew you loved her."

Thomas feels tears pricking at the backs of his eyelids. His uncle always seemed so gruff and unapproachable to him, but now he sees that it is all a facade. He has such a loving and compassionate heart. A heavy weight of regret settles on his heart when he thinks about all the years he lost, being raised to despise his uncle's very name. He feels compelled to share next.

"I didn't know Melissa very well, although I wish every day that I had gotten up the nerve to talk to her. Even just once, before she..." He takes a deep breath and lets it out slowly. "Anyhow, I remember the little things I could pick up without getting too close to her. Like, her skin was so perfectly white, but her hair was so dark black, like raven feathers. Melissa always seemed so frail, like the slightest breeze would turn her to dust. It is strange, though. I remember how she looked, acted, her little nervous habits. But I cannot remember her voice."

"You don't need every memory," Jas says quietly. "I can't remember Lisa's nervous habits. Isn't that strange? Certain aspects of those we love may fade, but others become more emphasized. Don't beat yourself up over this."

He nods, a large lump pressing against the inside of his throat. It feels good to talk about Melissa, to really force himself to think about her, but it is still so very painful. His uncle pushes back his chair to pace the kitchen.

"Helen loved to help others. She was always volunteering for some charity event, reading to kids with cancer, or walking dogs at the local humane society. Before she...before it happened, she was training for her first 5K. I remember how excited she was when she registered online. Her smile lit up the whole world."

He brushes away a few tears, staring out the window at a decaying garden. "I always tried to support her. I was selfish, and I wanted to spend more time with her, but this was what she was passionate about, you know? Helen was amazing. She could relate to anyone, anywhere, in any situation."

"I wish I could have met Aunt Helen."

"Me too, Tommy. She always wanted to meet you."

They stared at the table in silence, each of them fighting the urge to sob. So many things are beginning to change, mostly for the better. We can never go backward, no matter how desperately we try to live in the past. The future is all that awaits us, and we must greet it as it comes.

21

Everyone has more energy now that they are on the right track to discovering the rapist. It is crueler to be left in the dark than to see the end in sight and be able to fight for it, no matter the cost. Every step forward is a little victory in itself.

"I am positive that it is Liam Knotham." Thomas jabs a finger accusingly at the photo on the paper.

Jas patiently continues to highlight more obituaries, but his uncle releases a sigh of disapproval. "Tom, we cannot be sure yet. I'd love to say it is him and get him behind bars, but we have to be more careful."

"I agree with your uncle and with you, Tom. Liam seems like the likely suspect, but we can't just take a theory to court."

"I'm going to go grab Helen's old laptop." Jas and Thomas are surprised by this sudden impulse but remain silent. When he returns, he is talking rapidly. "I'll look into Liam's background. Maybe there are some files about him that could be used as evidence."

Thomas realizes that he should be helping Jas, but this is too intriguing. "Why didn't we think of this sooner?"

They ignore him until his uncle lets out a small cry of surprise. "He was divorced!"

Jas drops her highlighter like a bomb. "What? Let me see!"

The three of them crowd around the tiny screen and stare at the smug profile of Liam Knotham. His uncle reads aloud for them, giving them the highlights. "Looks like Liam was divorced twelve years ago. His wife was Nicole Baine, and they had one kid who stayed behind with his ex-wife."

Thomas cannot contain himself a moment longer. "That means his son is Asher!"

His uncle waves a hand to shut him up. "Anyhow, it seems possible. Looks like the mom felt that the divorce was too difficult for a four-year-old boy to understand, so she took custody of him and gave him her maiden name to cut off any connection to the father. Seems a bit suspicious if you ask me."

Jas seems to be in deep contemplation. "That would all make so much sense, though. If the son was four years old, and that was twelve years ago, then the child would be sixteen years old now. It all falls into place. Liam has to be the father of Asher Baine."

Thomas is nodding along with her. "It's a small town too, I mean, how many *Baines* can there be?"

"Don't go getting too excited about this," Benjamin points a finger in Thomas's face. "We need more concrete evidence."

It is so hard to not rush to the police. Thomas is more than convinced now that Asher's father is the rapist. But Liam did not rape Melissa, so does that mean Asher knew enough about his father to want to prove himself to him? He understands why Nicole would want to cut off any connections after going through a divorce, but in the meantime, was she hardening the child? Did the lack of communication with the only man in his life turn Asher into a violent child? Despite Thomas's currently rocky relationship with his own parents, he cannot imagine growing up without any father at all.

Jas seems especially uncomfortable with the discussion. She is pulling at the skin around her nails, sucking at the tiny droplets of blood that bubble up. It mystifies him for a moment before he realizes it must be a personal struggle. "Are you all right, Jas?"

She jumps slightly, nodding slowly before shaking her head instead. "Not really. It is petty but...after Lisa died, my parents got divorced. I was not enough to keep them together I guess. Anyhow, they're both remarried now, so great for them.

"My dad got remarried the proper way. He met a pretty little secretary at his office and proposed a few months later. But my mom...she already had a guy waiting for her. She was having an affair for who knows how long, and none of us even knew it."

She laughs bitterly, but the tears in her grey eyes cut it short. Thomas doesn't know what to do. He hates it when people cry. Should you hug them, touch them, lamely say it's all going to be okay when nothing ever will be?

"I don't want any pity," as if she can read his mind. "Apparently, I have an infant stepbrother now. I thought my mom couldn't have any more children, but clearly, that was just another lie. Someday, when he's older, I really want to meet him. But for now, I just can't go back. You understand that, right?"

"Totally."

"I figured you would."

"Wait, have you been homeless then?"

"Thomas, I can handle myself. I learned to grow up fast, and to be honest, the streets are much more welcoming than either of my homes could ever be."

How doleful of a world we live in that a paper box sodden by rain in an alley is more comforting than a home where we feel rejected. Is this how we want our children to be raised? To think that there is no place for them in this world, that they are nothing more than a spare piece to a puzzle which gets thrown away carelessly? Thomas opens his mouth to speak, but his uncle interrupts him. "Jas, you have a home here. I want you to feel welcome in my house, to finish school, to be a teenager who stays out late going to movies and school dances. You deserve to feel alive."

Can there ever be too much of a good thing? Clearly so, as Jas breaks down in sobs of what must be joy. She crumples to the floor like a rag doll. Benjamin kneels beside her, rubbing her back soothingly. "Helen and I could never have children." He looks up at Thomas. "So I'd be pretty happy if you two stuck around with this old man."

Thomas smiles at his uncle, this man whom everyone shuns, and for what? He is not someone evil or looking for a reward of some kind. No, all he wants is to make others feel loved in a world that believes love is defined by physical pleasures like money and sex.

Jas manages to speak, pushing a damp strand of hair out of her eyes. "I...I can't thank you enough."

"You don't have to thank me. I can't say this is a life of luxury, it is nowhere near perfect, but it is something."

"No," she shakes her head angrily. "Don't say that. It is perfect. It has love."

Everyone begins to cry, but it is not a shedding of pain. It is a release of holding themselves in. Their identities, their desires, their deepest thoughts, all forced to the surface in one beautiful emotion that cannot, and will not, be held back. Thomas has not felt such love, such wonderful pure love, in so long.

"All right," Jas commands, taking a deep breath. "Break is over, back to work."

Benjamin smiles like a proud father. "I'm on it."

He sits back down at the laptop, scrolling through reports of witnesses to the divorce, fees, and other inconsequential information. Thomas cannot help staring at Jas. How can someone who has gone through hell and back be so strong still? She seems to him like an invincible goddess immune to pain.

"What's wrong?" she murmurs.

Thomas realizes that his uncle's hand has frozen on the mouse as he stares at an enlarged photo of Liam Knotham. A vein pulses in his neck beside a red flush. He knows that a temper runs in his family, and he would rather not see his uncle's explosive rage.

Looking to Jas, he quietly beseeches her to fix the situation. In jest, she rolls her eyes. "Hey, Ben, how about we call it a day?"

He spins around to face her, and for one frightening moment, Thomas is worried he will hit Jas. Then his shoulders slump and he nods, obeying Jas like a little child. She reaches around him to close the laptop and cover up the disgusting image filling the screen.

"How about we go for a walk?" Thomas suggests.

"That sounds great." Jas's voice is too cheery to be natural, but he holds his tongue.

"Nah, I think I'll stay here. You two should go, though. It'll do you both good to get some fresh air in your lungs."

Thomas starts to protest, but Jas silences him with a venomous glare. They pull on some shoes before leaving the house.

"I feel bad for leaving him behind."

"It was his choice, Tom. I think he needs to be alone."

"For what? To break down, cry, and mourn alone? That has been his whole life, Jas."

"I know." She kicks a stone to tumble along the pavement. "But maybe that's just it. He has lived alone for so long now, that having a family is a foreign thing. Give him time to adjust."

They walk in silence for a while with no destination in mind. They pass several houses with tiny dogs yapping at the windows, bikes in the driveway, the lawn perfectly trimmed and green. Such normal families.

"You can't define normal."

Jas screws up her face. "Where did that come from?"

"No, really. Just stop and look around." He points across the street where a small boy is playing basketball while the parents get in a car to leave to attend some errand. The boy reluctantly puts down his ball, clearly not allowed to be outside when his parents aren't home.

"Is that normal, Jas? Yes, the family is together still. They have a nice house, two-car garage, and green lawn. Seems like they have it all together. The perfectly normal American family."

"What are you getting at?" She snaps impatiently.

"I mean, why is that our normal? Does normal strip us of our ability to love? We have to constantly prove to society that, hey, we are so totally normal in how we talk, dress, act, and live. We are so obsessed with this thing we call *normal* that we are slowly losing ourselves."

Jas just stares at Thomas for several heartbeats, making him wonder if he went too far. It is a thought that has flitted in and out of his mind for a while, but he has never felt it safe to voice those feelings out loud.

"You are right. I have felt similarly, but it just seems too weird to ignore what is normal. But...I guess that's kind of your point, huh?"

He laughs. "Yeah, I know what you mean, though. It is kind of my goal now to be the opposite of what the world thinks is *normal*."

"Me too." They share a small smile, and he feels like, once again, there are others in the world striving to find some good to cling to.

Suddenly, they find themselves at the bridge. The sky is clouding up, giving the scene an eerie aura. "We need to head back, it's getting late."

Thomas feels drawn to it. "Can't we just stay a little longer?" he whines.

"No!" She looks around nervously. "I'm leaving."

She gives him no choice but to follow, yet he is still unsure what scared her so much. It can't be the bridge itself as they have both come here before. He knows deep down that it is the pain of losing her sister, like visiting a haunted ghost. Talking about the memories was healing, but it only made the bridge more hateful.

They come home to find Benjamin raking the lawn. "You two are home early."

"The weather isn't looking so great," Jas lies quickly.

He doesn't seem convinced. "I suppose. Anyhow, there's hot chocolate on the stove if you want some."

Jas goes inside to warm up, but Thomas stays behind. He grabs a spare rake leaning against a tree to help his uncle.

"You don't have to do that, Tommy."

"But I want to." He pauses to glance up at his uncle through his bangs. "We are a family now."

His uncle smiles, a light in the gloomy day. "Yes, we are. Indeed, we are at last."

22

It feels like any lazy Sunday afternoon just spending time with his uncle. But it means the world to Thomas. Finding his family is more valuable than any earthly treasure.

"Hey, Tommy," Ben yells over the wind. "How about we go grab some of that hot chocolate with Jas?"

They leave their rakes in the shed, although it offers little protection from the elements. Rather, it seems to be growing another planet out of fungi on the inside. Thomas loves it; that smell of something old that cannot be moved.

Why does nothing last? His uncle is so sweet, so caring, and so good. It is now rare in our society to find anything close to the definition of good, that it becomes a precious artifact when we do happen to find. The irony is that while we search our lives for something good, we forget that we can be that good. If we are seeking goodness, so are others.

Someone needs to be the first one to change, and it often must start with ourselves.

Thomas has been trying to quench his insatiable anger. True, he knows that bad things happen to good people. What doesn't kill you makes you stronger, right? But that doesn't make it any more agreeable. It is still difficult to comprehend the pain of seeing someone we love being hurt.

Even now, though, the good is showing through. By the heinous act of Melissa and Helen's rape, the rapist may, at last, be captured and the past victims can receive the respect that they deserve. It is not always easy to do what is right, but if we don't, then what is left in this world to extinguish the darkness?

Asher must have wanted, no, *needed* to prove himself to his father. Thomas may be on shaky ground with his own family, but he knows how it feels to be inadequate to one's father. You are always looking for something to fill that void of longing. It does not mean that he forgives Asher.

How could he ever forgive him? To forgive is to forget, and Thomas vowed never to let himself forget a single piece of Melissa's life. For him, she is like a book, a rare and beloved novel. But then the idea of the novel was so grand that the author could not bear to finish it with a scant ending. Melissa is poetry: short, sweet, and utterly beautiful. She is mysterious but understood by only those who knew her heart. He misses her more and more every day, like a wound that won't scab over.

Thomas shakes himself out of his reverie lest his uncle grow suspicious. They found Jas sitting at her post at the kitchen table, steaming mug in one hand and a phone in the other. "Thank you so much, Nicole." She smiles as people do when they speak on the phone. How peculiar humans act at times. "Yes, I will stay in touch. Thanks again, bye now."

Why do we do that? Say bye *now*. It does not make any sense, but we still do it. Perhaps that is just how humans reason. Our lives are short and, unless we intervene, quite senseless at times. Thomas chastises himself for focusing on such petty details when there are much more pressing matters at hand.

"What did you find?"

"Well, I don't have your uncle's hacking skills, but I don't think I did too bad overall." Her smile is similar to the cat that ate the canary. "I was just on the phone with Nicole Baine."

Thomas is shocked. "*The* Nicole Baine?"

"The one and only. I found a stray file we must have overlooked about Liam's divorce. Apparently, there had been a report filed for physical abuse."

"That devil!" Benjamin slams his fist against the table, causing several highlighters to plummet. "Who did he abuse? His wife? His kid? Both?"

Jas holds up a hand in an attempt to calm his rage. "I didn't see any reports filed regarding Asher, but there were at least three filed in regards to Nicole."

Thomas digs his nails into his palms, relishing the stabbing pain. This is helpful, it adds up, makes sense. But as they learn more about this rapist, it only makes the acts he committed so much worse. How much torment did Helen endure? What causes every single one of his victims to end their lives? His stomach roils at what little Melissa went through.

"I wish Helen had told me..." Ben stifles a sob. "I could have helped her. I would have been there for her."

Jas is already shaking her head. "No, Ben. You did everything you could. She just had too many demons to fight."

"And she lost."

"She is at peace now, Ben."

"So, Nicole." Thomas hates seeming indifferent, but he is eager to know more. "What did she say?"

Jas seems disgruntled by his rude interruption. "She admitted that he would often beat her. Never to the point of hospitalization but sometimes pretty close. Nicole works at a children's hospital, and sometimes she would get home late and be exhausted after her shift. If she refused to have sex, well…"

She lets the sentence hang in the air. Ben's face is bright red, which Thomas is quite sure it is a mirror of his own complexion. He literally must have raped his own wife night after night after night. He treated her like nothing, using her only for his own pleasure.

Who knows how long this lasted? Their entire marriage, a few years, maybe weeks? Thomas cannot even begin to comprehend the fear of knowing that when you come home, you'll be beaten, used, and still be helpless. The courage Nicole must possess to have withstood it for so long is astounding.

"Anyhow," Jas continues. "I also managed to ask her if there was anything to do with an affair involved. Turns out there was."

She takes a deep breath, playing with the wireless phone in her hand. "You guys already know about how my parents are remarried. Since my mom was having an affair, that is kind of my first thought when someone mentions divorce. It sucks, but I can't help it. So it was on impulse that I asked her."

Benjamin leans against the counter. "What did she say?"

"Liam was having an affair." She cuts her eyes over to Thomas, seeking some stability in the storm. Her grey eyes are wide with some unknown terror that she is battling. "He, um, was having an affair for quite some time actually. Nicole said she would have ended the marriage anyhow due to this unfaithful act, but then..."

Her voice fades off as she nibbles a jagged nail. Thomas tries to be patient, but he himself is impatient. "But what, Jas?"

She turns to gaze at him, grey eyes unblinking. "He was having an affair with another man."

Benjamin makes a sound somewhere between a gag and a sob. Thomas feels his stomach roil in protest. What is wrong with this man, this animal? He is less than human, some beast that thinks of nothing other than satisfying his sexual nature. It certainly reveals why both genders were victims of the suicide bridge. How much horror this disgusting man has spread. For the first time since Melissa's death, Thomas is able to fully put himself in that place and imagine how it would feel. His heartbeat races at the thought of some man overpowering him to strip away his virginity.

He tries to force the image from his mind but fails. Does he even have a right to not think on it? After all, his torment is a nightmare never to be fulfilled. Melissa's torment was real. Immediately, Thomas feels like a coward for such selfish desires.

"How could he do that?" Ben pipes up. "I mean, two men...having..."

Thomas sees now that part of the reason his uncle is so disgusted by this news is that he cannot understand how two men can have sexual interactions. He does not want to cause tension or ill will, but he promised himself that he would always speak his mind. The change must start now, in ourselves.

"I do not support gay rights. But I won't tell someone how to live." His uncle glares at his nephew, an unseen wave of wrath held just beneath the surface. Thomas wipes a sweaty hand on his jeans. "Who has the power to judge? Well, God of course. But I am done condemning people for who they are. We go after every little issue in our society without focusing on the big things like catching a rapist. Why does our society seek to cause more pain when we should be healing our current wounds?"

"Indeed, Thomas. You are right again. I just cannot think rationally right now." He shakes his head miserably. "This is not love. No, this is rape. It is hate, greed, lust, anger all thrown together to form the hideous act of rape. I would bet anything that Liam did not love whatever man he was sleeping with. Someone like Liam Knotham is incapable of love, and I do not support rape."

Thomas dares to risk a glance at his uncle, standing stoically by the counter. His expression is a mask, giving no sign of anger but no sign of happiness either. He knows he went too far, but if we never cross that line, then what is our purpose? We are the only ones who can provide a voice to the voiceless, a hand to the helpless, and a home for the homeless. No good can ever come if we do not venture into the great unknown.

Benjamin lets out a long sigh. "You are right, yes, you are absolutely right." He pulls a bottle of brandy out of the cabinet nearest him and takes a swig of the amber liquid. "I never thought about how we just add to our pain. We need to heal. You helped me to see that clearer, Tommy.

"But this Liam guy...he didn't just rape people. He tore them apart, stole everything from them. Once he was finished, he left a shell behind. I just can't get my head around that. I just can't."

"It is awful how corrupt the world is." Jas stares at a distant point, though her mind seems to be somewhere else. "We judge everyone even though we hate to be judged. We try to please those who use us, and we ignore those who desire our friendship. Everything is turned upside down."

Thomas knows exactly how she feels. "Then we light the match."

She sniffs disdainfully. "Just until the pretty little world snuffs it out."

"No! We will fight."

Her hands shake from some caged-in emotion, and for a brief second, Thomas thinks she will make another objection. Then she nods, half her mouth turned up in a smile. "Then let us fight with courage."

Benjamin steps forward to pour his brandy down the sink. "We are fighters now."

23

The rest of Sunday passes in a blur. No one did much for the rest of the day. There was simply too much energy coursing through the air. They are fighters now. Fighting for a chance to bring light back into the world, to prove that goodness still exists.

The great philosopher, Immanuel Kant, had declared long ago in his essays that we should never get pleasure from doing good. Those things should be done from duty, no matter how we feel. Was that the reason they all were in such a turmoil of emotions lately?

Thomas could barely even remember going to bed, let alone falling asleep. Blacking out would be a more appropriate term to use. They were so close to avenging Melissa, to finally ending this torment. But it always seems to be just out of reach.

His head feels like it has been stuffed with cotton after being inflated two sizes too large. If this is what a hangover is like, why would anyone drink? While Thomas knows his splitting headache is not caused by intoxication, his high levels of exhaustion do not feel much better. The world spins when his feet hit the floor as his line of vision goes fuzzily to a black dot. He shuts his eyes, pressing two fingers against his temple to settle his nausea. A look at the clock says it is only five o'clock. He makes a mental note to talk to his uncle about getting a sleep med.

It is Monday. His stomach does a small flip. The weekend was such a nightmare that it seemed to go on for infinity. Now it is back to school, work, and reality. The world does not stop spinning when someone we love dies, and it certainly does not slow down even when we mourn.

Thomas wants to go back to bed. Back to the security and warmth of the heavy comforter where time does not seem to exist. Where if we are so lucky as to be blessed with sleep, we may dream of those we have lost. Reality has different ideas.

He plunges into the shower, not caring to adjust the heat and just letting the cold stream awake his skin. For twenty blissful minutes, nothing has to matter. There is a feeling to battle this numbness, something else to focus on. Once the skin of his hands starts wrinkling, he knows it is time to go. Reluctantly, he twists off the water, watching it disappear into the drain with all of his comfort with it.

It no longer matters how to dress, how to comb hair, or even to bother combing it at all. There certainly is no one to impress. If they choose to judge us based on appearances, they aren't worth it. The moment you wake up with messy hair, no makeup, baggy sweatshirt, that is *you*. If only the world could see that natural beauty is what is real, what matters.

Thomas rummages around in a kitchen drawer for some paper, finding a stack of neon green Post-it Notes. He grabs the nearest sharpie and scrawls a note that he is leaving for school and to call if anything happens.

His stomach is tying itself in knots, so he leaves without eating. If he suddenly feels hungry, he can eat at school, but he rather doubts it. There is too much to do today, and too much pressure to do it right.

Nothing has changed. The halls are still bustling with life, loud voices echoing off the cinder block walls. The fluorescent lights still flicker off and on. Teachers grade papers with the cursed red pen. Everything is the same.

Except for the empty chair, sitting beside a vacant desk. He closes his eyes to picture her there. Her raven black hair hiding her pale face in a cave, dark eyes focused on a book. She was more beautiful than any celebrity because she was naturally beautiful. It was like seeing the sunrise. You had to care enough to make an effort to see the beauty before it disappears, but there will never be anything quite like it.

He feels like a ghost traveling between classes, taking tests, just going through the motions. Only when the final bell rings does he finally feel alive. His whole body is shaking, whether from exhaustion, hunger, or anticipation. Probably all three.

Asher and his friends mingle out in the hall, leaning against their lockers. A ringing fills his ears. Thomas has never felt so angry in his entire life. Perhaps not even this angry when he first heard about Liam Knotham. Asher actually raped Melissa, and he doesn't even care. It was all just a game to him.

"Hey!" Thomas yells. They don't seem to hear him, or else they don't care. Asher tells another crude joke which makes them all burst out laughing. Thomas feels heat creeping up his neck. "I was talking to you, you ugly pig."

This gets Asher's attention. "What'd you call me?"

"An ugly pig." Thomas dares to step closer. "But I think that would be an insult to pigs, now wouldn't it?"

One of Asher's friends slams Thomas against a locker. "Shut up! What's all this about anyway?"

He smells like sweat and cheap aftershave. Thomas spits in his face. "He raped Melissa. He raped her and he..."

His rant is cut off by a hard punch across the jaw. A trickle of blood drips off of Thomas's lip. It tastes like salt and metal. It is time; there may not be another chance ever again. He slips a hand into his pocket and flips the switch.

The tiny recorder hums to life. Thomas smiles despite his broken lip. Asher stares at him like he's gone mad. "Huh, your dead girlie really screwed you up didn't it?"

Thomas tried to swing at Asher, but he is slow and clumsy. "Don't...don't call her that!"

"She was pretty fun to play with, you know," Asher smirks maliciously. "Pity she never allowed my friends to get a turn."

Thomas realizes that fighting is futile. These are stuck-up jocks, good for nothing besides their brute strength. He will have to fight this battle with words rather than actions.

"Why did you rape her?"

"Why? Well, she wasn't *bad* looking, and I was bored."

Thomas's blood begins to boil, and he is forced to swallow a string of heated retorts. "So you really just decided to rape a thirteen-year-old girl for absolutely no reason."

Asher shrugs indifferently. "Sure. I mean, why not? She always kinda dressed slutty. Short skirts and whatnot. Melissa was asking for it."

That stops Thomas short. He remembered her name, this meant something to him. But not regret. No, Melissa had been a reward, a prize. She was a name to put to his action; something to be proud of, as disgusting as it may be.

Thomas decides to go out on a limb. "What does your father think of this? Or have you not even told your parents yet?"

Asher's face becomes guarded at the mention of his father. Clearly, a nerve has been struck. "I am sure my father knows."

It is Thomas's turn to smile now. "What makes you so sure of that?"

"None of your business, now is it?" Asher moves dangerously closer. "You need to learn to talk less, or maybe I can arrange that for you."

He slams a fist into Thomas's gut, making him double over in pain. One of his friends slams a hand into his ear, making the floor tilt. Through his slitted eyes, he sees people slowing down in the hallway to watch, but no one even attempts to help him. No one ever wants to get involved.

"Melissa was a slut, got it?" Asher pressed his fingers against Thomas's throat, causing him to gasp for breath. "She deserved far more than she got. I certainly got some pleasure out of it. Can't imagine why she didn't."

His arrogance fuels fresh rage in Thomas. He slams his head against Asher, probably hurting himself more in the process but equally satisfied with his efforts. "Maybe she just doesn't like ugly, stupid, gross animals. Maybe she was just appalled by your lack of intelligence. After all, she was a genius, and you are not even human so..."

"Shut UP!" Asher roars. Thomas's insults are petty, but it is enough to spark some more rage, which is just what he wanted. "I should've killed her myself, but I guess she saved me the trouble by taking the leap."

Hatred bubbles up in Thomas's chest. "How could you? She was so young!"

"They are always more fun when they're young. I mean, hey, she hadn't even been used yet."

"How could you?" Thomas repeats incredulously.

"I didn't have a choice," Asher growls. For the first time, he has a hint of frustration in his eyes. "It was something I had to do, and I would do it again gladly."

"That is a lie, it's all lies!" Thomas spits. "You should have died too."

No more words are exchanged as Asher and his friends pummel Thomas until he is broken and bloody. They back away at last, Asher leaving with an obscene gesture in Thomas's direction.

He lays there on the tile floor, his back pressed against the cold metal of the lockers. Then he laughs. Students walk by him faster, casting worried glances over their shoulders as he collapses in laughter. He pulls the tiny recorder out of his pocket and presses the off button.

If only they knew. They caused him temporary pain, but he now holds the power to ruin their lives. Going back to the beginning of the tape, he presses play to listen to their confessions once again. Another bubble of laughter escapes his lips. He did it. Finally, he has done something right.

He stumbles to his feet, his legs shaking from the fight. The smile never leaves his face, though. This is the next step of condemning Asher and his father. The police can listen to this evidence being spoken straight from Asher Baine himself. Thomas cannot believe his good fortune, a blaze of courage burning in his soul.

24

The walk from school takes longer as he limps along the sidewalk. If he was uninjured, there would certainly be a spring in his step. As it is, he begins to see everything in a lighter mood, his spirits lifted tremendously by this sudden breakthrough. He opens the door and greets his uncle cheerfully. Benjamin steps into the living room, recoiling in shock. "Thomas, what in the world?"

Jas joins them, her face a reflection of Benjamin's. "Thomas, what happened to you? Are you okay?"

Thomas laughs at the ridiculousness of the question. Clearly, he is not physically okay. Mentally, however, he feels better than he has in days. The bruises covering his arms are proof of his success.

"I confronted Asher and his friends again today," he pronounces with a sense of pride.

"What do you mean by *again?*" His uncle's rage seems about to explode any second now.

"I forgot to tell you guys," Thomas wrings his hands regretfully. "But, um, before I got kicked out of my house, I had gotten a broken lip from Asher."

Jas is nodding her head slowly. "I remember. You had walked into the store dripping wet with blood running down your chin."

"Oh, yeah. I forgot."

"It's cool." She carves a line in the table with her thumbnail. "Still, you can't be so rash all the time. I get it, you're super young and impulsive, but Asher could've killed you."

"Super young? Impulsive? What do you think, Jas, that I was just trying to pick a fight at school? This was all for Melissa." He gestures to the myriad of cuts and bruises now turning a sickly shade of yellow. "I know how Asher is. I *did* think this through, and I would do it all over again in a heartbeat."

He pauses, waiting for her to say something. The room seems to be holding its breath. "I'd die for her, Jas."

Benjamin must have left while they were arguing, now returning with a few damp cloths. "Clean yourself up and start explaining. Now."

Thomas sees that it is futile to fight. "I had sort of been considering this for a while. You know, talking to them again." Pressing the cloth against the cuts stings like fire, but it is something else to focus on. "When we had gone back to my house, I brought my tiny voice recorder with me, figured it might come in handy. Anyhow, when I confronted them, I turned it on."

He allows himself a brief smile of satisfaction. "They had no idea. Asher spilled all his secrets, and his friends backed him up like the sickly loyal losers that they are." All of the pent-up hatred begins pouring out at once in a sudden wave of emotions. "I barely even felt their blows. They raped her like it was a game, a contest, some sort of dare. Melissa was just a prize, a trophy for Asher to say he had *won*. I got it all. All of it is on this recorder."

Proudly, he pulls the recorder out of his pocket to pass to his uncle. Benjamin just shakes his head in disbelief. "As much as I want to punish you for being an idiot, Tommy...I can't." He claps his nephew on the shoulder. "This is incredible, Thomas. You did the right thing, even though it was difficult."

Thomas feels a warm glow spreading through his body. So this must be what fatherly approval feels like. Unconditional love and acceptance. A feeling of pride even when some things were wrong. No judgment, just pure love.

It is a hard path, narrow and twisting with no clear end. But every day, something else will begin to make sense; one more piece added to the infinite puzzle of life's mystery. We always want all the answers at once, but sometimes, we have to stop and let the questions come first before anything can be solved.

25

The clock on the wall reads five in the evening, with the October sun preparing for bed. A masterpiece of color is painted across the sky in pinks, oranges, and purple. For the first time in days, maybe even weeks, Thomas can appreciate this profound beauty. Instead of sadness, he feels joy in knowing that Melissa would have found it beautiful too.

Benjamin sinks into the armchair beneath the window, the last rays of light highlighting his grey hairs. "I want to get this information to the police as soon as we can, but it is getting very late. How about we turn it in tomorrow bright and early?"

Before Thomas can even begin to protest, Jas jumps off the couch. "No! We cannot wait any longer. Waiting is what killed Lisa, Helen, and Melissa. Every other victim could have been saved if someone had known and acted when they were witnessing the rape."

"She's right, Uncle Ben." An aura of tension hangs in the space. "Besides, we'll never sleep until it's done."

"Fine," he relents with a sigh of old age. "I'm not as young and full of energy as you two, so you have to understand when I am slower. But I can see both of your points, and I agree with you guys. Tonight we shine a light in the darkness."

Jas materializes next to Thomas dressed to go outside. "How did you get ready so fast?"

"Once you started your little speech, I had a hunch we'd be going."

They share a secret smile. It is not the first time Thomas has wished that Jas was his sister. How amazing it would be to have someone so close to you who understands and cares about you. If only she would stay with them permanently. It seems as if she might, but for now, getting high hopes will only cause more pain.

The car's headlights blaze a trail through the murky evening. Thomas cannot sit still. He plays with the recorder like a little kid, unable to put it away. Benjamin glances over. "Tommy, leave that thing be. It'd be hell to pay if that thing got erased."

Immediately, he pulls his hands back. Erasing that recorder would be an absolute nightmare. He would not only be failing Melissa but also Lisa, Helen, and every other victim of the bridge. Why is he always so careless?

The rest of the drive is passed in silence. A few trees shiver from the stiff breeze while the rest of the world waits in anticipation. This could be the tipping point. There is really no reason why the police shouldn't help them, but still, no one is eager to be disappointed.

"We are here," Benjamin announces to the car.

Jas jumps out, bouncing on the balls of her feet. For some reason, this simple act annoys Thomas. "Why are you so eager?"

She shrugs. "I don't know. It's like I finally feel something. I guess I am finally feeling alive again."

Thomas just nods, but it is enough for them to realize that they are sharing that feeling of knowing what it means to be alive. Not just living a daily routine of eating, breathing, and sleeping but to feel something and express emotions. It is as if a window has been opened, and they can finally see the horizon. They have hope now.

The sign on the door says it closes in ten minutes, but Jas marches inside anyway. A police officer behind a desk flooded with papers looks up in exasperation. "We close in ten minutes."

Jas is literally glowing with energy. "Yeah, saw that. But you are open now, and you are going to want to see this."

Thomas goes to stand beside Jas. "She's right. This is a recording of a sixteen-year-old boy named Asher Baine who recently raped Melissa Downs."

This seems to pique the officer's attention. "The Downs girl, huh?" He narrows his eyes at Thomas. "So tell me then, how did you get this recording? Were you involved too?"

Benjamin pulls Thomas back before he can punch the man in the jaw. "I'm his uncle, and I can tell you right now that none of us were involved. All of us here have lost someone to rape. We just want to bring our loved ones some justice, officer."

"Let me listen to it while you guys take a seat." He indicates some plastic chairs against a far wall.

Thomas wants to protest so he can stand there the entire time. Jas obeys first, and Benjamin's insistent pull on Thomas's arm forces him to follow as well. The plastic chairs have no give, resulting in an awkward posture. It is as if whoever designed them wanted the user to be as uncomfortable as possible.

The clock on the wall ticks off every minute loudly, adding to his increasing anxiety. No way is that recording more than ten minutes long, yet it feels as though hours have passed. Perhaps the officer wanted to replay it, or more likely, he simply forgot they were even there.

"You guys can come back over."

Jas springs up, covering the distance to the desk in four long strides. Benjamin and Thomas linger a bit longer, wanting to keep the officer waiting like he did for them. The recorder has been turned off and is now resting in a sealed plastic bag marked *evidence* in black sharpie.

"I will admit, there is some pretty convicting stuff on that tape." Thomas notices that the officer's name is Walter Cramoors by the plaque on his desk. "Still, I need to hear the full story from you before I can send it in for further investigation."

It is Jas's turn to be shocked. "What? Why aren't you investigating this now? It's all right there!"

Walter ignores her, picking up the phone next to a mountain of manila folders. "Hey Dan, can you come down to the lobby?" He listens to the voice on the other end of the receiver, one finger raised for silence. "Sounds good, yup, thanks."

"What was that all about?"

"Girl, you need to show more respect."

Thomas slams his hand against the desk, sending a tower of papers fluttering to the ground. "Don't you dare talk to her like that again!"

Benjamin casts a warning glare at Thomas. "I think we all just need to calm down a bit. I apologize for the rude behavior on my nephew's part, Officer Cramoors. But I must say, I, too, would like to know what is to be done with the recording."

Cramoors looks livid, his eyes burning with hatred. "Once my colleague, Dan Waters, gets down here, everything will be explained."

On cue, a heavyset man with salt and pepper hair enters the room, a mug of coffee clutched in one hand and a tablet in the other. "Are these the folks, Walter?"

"These are the ones." He tosses Dan the recorder, causing Thomas's heart to jump into his throat. "This is their evidence."

If Walter Cramoors was rude before, he is absolutely intolerable now. The presence of the other police officer seems to have only heightened his arrogance. However, rather than go along with the snarky demeanor, Dan Waters frowns thoughtfully. "Be more careful, Walt. This is important, and I won't have you trashing another case."

Walter's face turned crimson as he fumbles with some random papers. Thomas is allowed to be the one smiling now. He is liking Dan Waters more and more.

"Thomas confronted Asher Baine for that information," Jas declares rather proudly. "Just to add, Asher is also the son of Liam Knotham and Nicole Baine. Based on all the evidence we found, Liam is the rapist, and Asher raped Melissa in an attempt to get his father's approval."

"That sounds so accurate, I'm letting myself believe it." Dan Waters makes eye contact with Jas. "But for now, until we can prove it without a doubt, it is still a theory."

Jas huffs in frustration. "But it makes so much sense.."

"I agree that it does. Once I listen to this, I'll hear the full story from all of you, and we can go from there."

"Do you want us to go sit over there again?" Thomas gestures sarcastically at the row of plastic chairs.

Dan looks confused. "No, why would I do that?"

Walter's ears turn an even deeper shade of red, much to Thomas's satisfaction. He keeps his gaze locked on Cramoors. "I was just curious."

However, Dan is no longer listening. He is holding the tiny recorder carefully next to his ear as though he is worried about missing a single second of it. His eyes widen off and on, and a vein pulses in his neck. After a long ten minutes, he shuts off the recorder and stares at the three of them.

"Tell me everything."

26

Thomas is elated by the officer's enthusiasm. This is more than he could've hoped for, and once again, everything feels like it is falling into place. As much as he wants to have the lead of telling the story, he knows that Jas possesses the most crucial information of all.

"You should tell the story."

She looks startled. "Why me?"

"You know more than any of us. You actually talked to Nicole." He gives her hand a quick squeeze. "I believe in you."

Jas takes a deep breath to collect herself, letting it out slowly. "All right, then." She turns to face Officer Waters. "Thomas is right; I did talk to Nicole on the phone. She divorced Liam Knotham twelve years ago, which is why she chose to keep her maiden name. They had a son, Asher Baine, who was four years old at the time of the divorce.

That's why the rapings all make sense in that regard because the first suicide for rape was reported four months after the day Liam was divorced."

She continues to tell the story in a monotone voice as though she is giving a documentary. "Anyhow, Nicole also mentioned that Liam was often abusive. If she, um, refused to have sex with him, he would beat her. She worked long hours as a nurse for a children's hospital, and she took that abusive treatment every single night for who knows how long." She shakes her head in disbelief. "She is such a strong woman."

"Anyhow, Thomas connected the dots that Asher was estranged from his father and wanted a way to prove himself to him. In his sick mind, he believed that his father would be proud if he, too, raped a girl. So Asher raped Melissa, and Liam raped all of the other victims of the bridge." She looks to Thomas for confirmation. "And that brings us here today."

Thomas is awestruck by how calm Jas is. He feels like a bundle of nerves. Dan is nodding, but Walter looks positively amused. His voice sounds lined with laughter. "So, what does this prove exactly?"

"It proves that Liam is the rapist," Jas insists. "He already had an abusive record."

"That's quite enough, Cramoors," Dan chides, fixing him with a look. He turns back to Jas. "I believe you, and it does all make sense. But I won't rush this. I'd like to get another witness or someone else who knew him in here."

"That could be arranged, officer," Ben interjects smoothly.

"For when?" Thomas explodes. He has been holding it in too long. "We need to act now!"

"Tommy, calm down right now."

His uncle's tone sends a clear warning to shut up and stay quiet, but Thomas ignores it. "No, I won't." His rebellious retort surprises even himself. "Melissa could have been saved by acting sooner. We cannot wait, we literally have to move now!"

"Thomas, I mean it, be quiet! I will *not* tell you a third time."

He feels like a child now, stamping his foot when he doesn't get everything his way. It is just so frustrating to see the end so near in sight and be totally helpless to do anything about it. Jas is standing stock still, gazing off into nothingness.

"He is right, though. We cannot wait." Her voice radiates calm. "However, if we have the time, why not act now?"

Dan sighs, glancing at the clock ticking merrily away on the wall. "Who would you call?"

Benjamin snaps his fingers. "I've got it. The newspapers, what was it called...the *Clermont Observer*! Liam wrote the obituaries for the paper, which is how we found him because he never once published an obituary for a rape victim."

"So, who are you insinuating I call?"

"The owner of the paper," Ben speaks slowly as if this should be completely obvious. "Just call the paper and ask for the owner."

"After you call, will you send someone to arrest Knotham?" Thomas demands, forgetting the rule of silence.

Dan sighs. "Look, kid, evidence takes time to stack up, okay? If everything keeps falling into place so nicely, maybe we can nab the guy within a week or so. These cases don't usually proceed too quickly."

Thomas closes his mouth for once while the officer calls the newspaper. Miraculously, they are still open. Dan steps off to the side and speaks in hushed tones before replacing the phone in his pocket. "The owner is Carter Mason. He seems pretty shaken up, but he should be stopping by shortly."

"Calm down, Tommy." He feels himself blush at his uncle's chiding, shocked that he could read Thomas's mood so easily. Suddenly, a door next to a hallway opens and a third officer appears.

His skin is a rich brown like melted chocolate, and his head is cleanly shaven. Despite his pleasant smile, his eyes look confused. "Dan, Walter," he starts, his voice thickly accented. "Why haven't you two clocked out yet?"

Walter just sneers. "Ask the kid, why don't you? He never shuts up anyhow."

"Well neither do you, so maybe you should start learning right about now."

Jas giggles nervously, then gets herself back under control. Thomas is liking this new officer more and more. Dan just shrugs before taking a sip of his now cold coffee. "I was actually coming down to do just that when these three showed up. They've got a pretty interesting case with some evidence, and I couldn't just walk away, Malik."

Thomas now sees that his name tag reads Malik Holmes. He feels a sense of warmth for Officer Waters for staying late to help them out. A prick of guilt settles in his stomach for his rude behavior in rushing forward.

Officer Holmes nods thoughtfully. "How are you proceeding now then?"

"I called the local newspaper and the owner, Carter Mason, is dropping by soon."

"Someone better catch me up to speed then."

All eyes turn to Jas, making her smile bashfully. "I'd be happy to."

27

Officer Holmes tells them all to sit down so they can wait for Carter Mason to arrive. "In the meantime, I'd be more than happy to have you tell me your story."

Jas looks more confident this time. "I am sure you have heard of the suicide bridge, and that those victims took their own lives because they had been raped." She glances up from her lap to make sure he is following. "Well, we believe that we have found the rapist.

"His name is Liam Knotham, and he works for the *Clermont Observer,* which is why Carter Mason is coming. Anyhow, he had gotten divorced around twelve years ago, and the first suicide victim was reported just four months after. I called his wife, Nicole Baine, which linked everything back to Asher Baine, who had raped Melissa."

She pauses for breath, so Malik uses the opportunity to voice a question. "Do you know why they got divorced?"

"Liam was abusive. If Nicole refused to, you know, have sex with him, he would beat her. She worked as a nurse for a children's hospital, so she usually came home exhausted. Honestly, I wish I was as strong as Nicole."

"Hey, wait," Dan pipes up. "Why didn't the kid, what's his name? Asher? Why didn't he keep his father's name if he wanted to prove himself so much?"

"Nicole told me that it was her choice for Asher to use her maiden name. Since he was only four years old, growing up with no father in the home, she decided it would be best to erase all memory of Liam, starting with his name. While that might not have been the best choice, it was her only option at the time."

"Well, I'll be." Malik lets out a low whistle. "I wonder how long she put up with that demon."

Thomas feels joy in having found another teammate. Despite the other two officers having lingering doubts, Officer Holmes is clearly on their side. A knock at the door makes them all jump.

"Hang on." Walter types in a code on a security panel. "I forgot the doors lock automatically."

"What don't you forget," Milak mumbles.

A middle-aged man with thinning red hair walks in. His face is so pale that every freckle stands out like a star in a galaxy. Thomas takes in his khaki pants and white dress shirt, knowing that this must be Carter Mason.

"Please, officers, I am not a bad person. I never knew I had anyone like that working for me, I swear that..."

Milak holds up a hand to cut him off. "No one is blaming you, Mr. Mason. We just want to talk."

"He seems like a little imbalanced," Jas whispers to Thomas.

He nods in reply, taking in the character of Carter Mason. Since the moment he stepped inside, his hands have been twitching nervously, while his eyes dart around searching for some unseen threat. His nervous demeanor has even set Thomas on edge.

"What do you, um, want to talk about?"

Dan leans his elbows on the desk, a folder perching precariously on the corner. "What do you know about Liam Knotham?"

Carter's shoulders relax immediately. "Liam? That's easy enough because there is really nothing to him. He always shows up on time for work, but he's part-time so he isn't there every day. Basically, all he does is write the obituaries for us."

"What is his attitude like?"

"Oh gosh, Liam is as sarcastic as they come. He always has some snide remark. But all in jest, all in jest. I don't know if I've ever seen him serious."

"I cannot believe it," Dan slams the desktop. "It was all just an act. One big, stupid act."

Carter looks confused, his eyes getting a fearful hint in them. "An act? What's an act? By who?"

"Liam was fooling everyone," Jas informs him in a low voice as if soothing a frightened child. "See, Liam was a rapist, but we need more witnesses to really finalize the evidence. We knew he wrote obituaries for your paper, and what I want to know is why you never published them all."

"What?" Carter's voice has lost its nervous tremor. "Young lady, I publish *everything*. I am very passionate about writing, and I believe every writer should be given a chance to make their mark. No, you are mistaken. Nothing was ever not published."

Benjamin drops a stack of unpublished obituaries in his lap. "How about those then?"

His brow furrows as he reads them. "Liam wrote these?" He looks up at their faces. "I never knew about these, I swear. Every day before he leaves, he hands me a list with all the obituaries checked off to show me that he did all his work. I just assumed that he had low self-esteem but now…"

"Now you realize he was hiding the truth," Jas finishes for him.

"How can this be? I'm an honest man. I have always believed in working hard and being truthful. I…I just…"

Carter buries his face in his hands. Thomas is unsure whether this outburst of emotion is from the horror of what Liam did, or the disgrace the paper is suffering. Finally, he slides his hands down to his neck, sighing in misery. "Well, you must have the right guy obviously. But tell me, what did Liam do exactly that has you so interested?"

"He has raped countless victims who took their own lives at the bridge," Thomas doesn't care if he is too blunt. "His son, Asher, raped Melissa Downs, a young, beautiful girl from my school. His wife divorced him twelve years ago for abuse." He pauses to let Carter take in the information. "So the reason I am interested, Mr. Mason, is because I want him thrown in jail for the rest of his miserable life."

"I never would have hired him if I had known."

"Don't go beating yourself up," Malik consoles him. "He was crafty, literally destroying our community right in front of our eyes."

"We certainly have a lot of good evidence to go by," Dan says in an attempt to boost their spirits.

Thomas ignores him, addressing only Officer Holmes. "So what do we do know?"

"Now," he reaches into his back pocket for a cell phone, "I am going to call Nicole Baine and settle this case."

28

J as leans closer to Thomas while Officer Holmes makes the call. "Do you think they will arrest just Liam, or Asher too?"

"If it was me, I'd have them killed."

"Again, you are so young and rash. You know that will never, and *should* never, happen."

"Why not?"

She throws her hands up in the air. "Because it is inhumane, Thomas. It is too severe."

"Oh, but raping someone and causing them to kill themselves suddenly is humane."

"Think about who you want to be. Do you want to be just like Asher? Full of ugly hate and lies and misery? Or would you rather be the change this world needs to show love even to enemies and do what's right?"

She turns slightly, leaving him to ponder these thoughts alone. He grits his teeth until he cannot stand the ache, which only makes him clench his jaw harder. As much as he does not want to admit it, Jas has a point. Does he *really* want to be like Asher? If there is to ever be any change at all, someone has to be different.

He leans his head against the cold wall, sighing heavily. "Okay, you were right. I'm sorry."

She stares at him with her lips pursed. "Good. More than likely they will both spend some jail time. Liam will get the heavier sentence, and don't be surprised if they let Asher off the hook completely. Remember, he is a minor still."

Thomas clenches his hand to contain his anger. Minor or not, what Asher did was wrong. Instead, he tucks his thoughts away so that Jas won't be angry. "That's true. I guess we just have to wait and see."

"We sure do a lot of waiting, huh?"

They both turn to look as Milak finishes his call. He slips the phone back in his pocket before turning to face them. "Nicole is glad that you guys took on the case. She has not heard from Liam these last twelve years, but Asher always asked about his father apparently. She is...she's quite heartbroken about the whole matter."

"A mother will always stand by her son," Benjamin agrees.

Milak seems surprised by Benjamin's agreeable demeanor. "That is true I suppose."

"Hey guys," Dan gets their attention. "I found Liam's address. 947 Samson Street."

"Are we arresting him for sure?" Walter wonders.

Officer Holmes runs a hand tiredly over his face, making Thomas wonder what time his day started. "Let me call my wife to tell her I'll be late and then...yeah. We have to arrest Liam Knotham and Asher Baine."

Thomas jiggles his foot impatiently while Milak calls his wife, Tonya. They are finally getting somewhere. All the hours of hard work and heartache have paid off, and Melissa can be avenged at last. He shares an excited half smile with his uncle, but when he turns towards Jas, he sees that she is scowling. "Hey, what's up?"

"How is this helping Melissa? Or Lisa? Or Helen or any of the victims?"

"Jas, come on, don't do this." He reaches for her hand, but she pulls back. Thomas feels like he's been slapped. "They would have wanted this to end. I know for a fact that Melissa would never have wanted anyone else to endure what she went through."

"I guess so," Jas whispers to her shoes. "I just wish I could do something bigger. Something that really matters."

"Trust me, this is something big."

Before she can reply, Milak walks back over to them. "I can't have you guys along; there isn't any room in the squad car anyhow. But I'll leave it up to you whether you'd like to wait here or go home."

"We will wait here," Benjamin decides for them.

Milak is already nodding. "That's what I figured. All right, we should be back within the hour."

With that, Officers Holmes and Waters leave the station. Walter props his feet on the desk, watching something on the computer. Benjamin paces the room, and Jas seems more distant than ever, so Thomas is alone with his thoughts. When was the last time Asher and his father were together? Was it really twelve years ago? It is somewhat ironic that the two would be reunited in a squad car. Thomas almost laughs at the thought, his nerves are so high.

The forty minutes spent waiting pass in complete silence. No one knows what to say as they wait for the officers to arrive. It's like the entire world is holding its breath, unsure whether to dread their arrival or to long for the wait to be over.

At last, the squad car pulls up, lights flashing red and blue. Thomas feels a sadistic sense of pleasure when he sees Asher sobbing. Suddenly, he no longer appears as the bully everyone believes him to be. With his face red and streaked with tears, he is more pathetic rather than tough.

Liam, however, looks downright smug. He shows absolutely no affection for Asher, treating his own son worse than you would a stranger. Benjamin leans over to speak in Thomas's ear. "I almost feel bad for the kid. Imagine having a father like that."

Thomas says nothing because he does not agree. He feels no pity for Asher. How could anyone ever feel pity for someone who is a rapist? Other people have had rough starts in life and still led good lives. He is not about to give Asher a break just because he had an absent father.

The crimes Asher committed against Melissa can never be erased. He stole her identity, her virginity, and her life. Thomas is irritated that his uncle would even consider offering Asher any pity. He turns to Jas to gauge her reaction.

"Hey, how are you doing?"

She shrugs. "Probably the same as you. Confused, relieved, sad, just all messed up."

"I feel exactly the same way." He looks at her downcast face. "But, we can at least know that we are doing the right thing."

Jas hesitates briefly before nodding in agreement. "You're right. But why doesn't it feel right?"

"I think it is because everything is becoming so final. We had a purpose to find whoever raped all those people, and now that we've succeeded, we don't know what to do with ourselves."

"That about sums it up."

Officer Holmes approaches their little group. "Well, they're both locked up for now until further questioning. As of now, Knotham is going to be given the max sentence for rape, thirty years. Since Asher is a minor, we are charging him with five years in juvie."

It does not satisfy Thomas's thirst for revenge, but he swallows his complaints. This is more than they could have hoped for. At last, both of the rapists are getting what they deserve and will be punished accordingly and humanely.

Thomas is surprised by how much this experience has forced him to mature. He allows himself to smile before shaking Milak's hand. "Thank you, sir, for everything."

29

Milak pulls a plastic chair closer to them and sits down heavily. He smiles at each of them, bringing some cheer to the gloomy setting. "I want to thank all of you for what you've done here. It means more to me than you can imagine."

Benjamin crosses his arms comfortably. "You're welcome, officer. I bet it's never easy having to hunt down a rapist."

Wiping his brow, he sighs. "No, Ben, it isn't. Rapists are crafty devils, and Knotham sure wasn't an exception."

"I'm just glad everyone is safe at last," Ben shakes his head in relief.

Thomas can't just let the adults do all the talking. "But we were still too late, weren't we? I mean, think of all the countless victims that monster raped."

Benjamin glares at Thomas, but Milak just waves his hand dismissively. "Let him speak his mind, Ben. It'll do him more good than keeping all of that anger inside." He shifts in his seat to face Thomas directly. "For the record, I agree with you one hundred percent. I am the child of a rape, so I know firsthand how evil it is."

Thomas stares back at Milak's kind face in shock. "You mean your mother was...?"

"Raped? Yes, she was. Like Melissa, she was also very young. Only 15 years old when he raped her. That's why I was sent up for adoption and was taken in by an amazingly loving family."

"Did you ever get to meet your mother?" Jas whispers.

"I have, and she is just as sweet as I could've imagined. She had been feeling so guilty for sending me off to be adopted, and I am so glad she got to meet my new family, so she could see that she did the right thing."

He swipes at a few stray tears, making Thomas choke up slightly. Jas lets out a strange squeak before breaking down. How much pain did this one man cause? It feels like nothing will ever change after all because the scars will never fade. The world doesn't care how much you try, or how much you've had to lose because we are insignificant variables that can always be replaced.

"I know that sometimes it feels like it will never get better," Milak seems to be reading Thomas's mind. "But things are slowly improving. Look around, the rapists are caught, you found new friends, and I got an amazing family."

"But what did it cost?" Jas chokes out, wiping her nose on her coat sleeve.

"Everything. But that's what makes it worth it."

Benjamin clears his throat several times. "When my wife, Helen, was raped, I didn't know what to do. I just kind of kept my distance, like I was taking care of a scared animal." He sniffs disdainfully. "So when she went to the bridge...I felt like I had failed her somehow. If I had been there more, done something, *anything*, maybe she would still be alive.

"But then you came to my house, Tommy, and I saw how wrong I had been. You sought me out because your family shunned you, so you needed an old outcast like me. You gave me a purpose and a new family." He smiles through his tears at Thomas and Jas. "Helen spent her life serving others, and I swear I'll do the same for as many years as I have left in me."

"They inspire us don't they?" Jas whimpers.

Thomas ponders this for a moment. Through their death, they bring us hope. We never know what we have until it's gone, so we must seize every opportunity as it comes. Tomorrow is never promised, but today is always a gift.

"Melissa saw beauty in dark places." Thomas is a bit reluctant to share such an intimate memory, but this is how healing happens. "I'd see her doodling on a notebook in dark pen. Sometimes it just looked like a scrawled mess, like some gothic art. But then I saw human figures, more elegant than anything I'd seen before, blooming from the tip of her pen. Once, she entered a painting at school in a contest and got last place. It was all greys, white, and black, but it was beautiful. She took death and brought it to life. She...she took away the fear."

Jas is crying still, but there is an expression of joy on her face. "That is perfect, Thomas." She shakes her head, a few tears landing on her hands. "I really wish I could have known her."

"She sounds like an amazing girl," Milak agrees.

Carter Mason walks towards them, escorted by Officer Waters. He is no longer wringing his hands, and his voice holds more confidence now. "I am truly sorry for all of the pain you have endured. I cannot imagine how you must be feeling, and I know that words can seem insignificant in times like this. However, I hope you'll allow me to write a section in my paper dedicated to the victims of the suicide bridge. I will certainly highlight how miraculous Melissa, Lisa, and Helen were. But only with your permission."

"I would love for Helen to be remembered. It...it would be like paying a last respect that was never given." He shakes Carter's hand firmly, tears of joy filling his eyes. "Thank you, sir. This is really wonderful of you."

"It is my absolute pleasure, Ben. Oh, and please, call me Carter?"

"Thank you, Carter."

"Lisa would have been thrilled to be in the paper. I think this will be a good ending before another beginning."

Carter squeezes her hand sympathetically. "That is lovely, Jas, thank you."

All eyes are now turned toward Thomas, eagerly awaiting his answer. He feels conflicted regarding his current options. Melissa deserves to be remembered, she deserves to be honored and respected, but does the world deserve to know her like that? They never cared when she was alive, why should they get to know her in death?

Still, this is more than he will ever be able to do for her. Yes, he did help to get Asher convicted, but what had he done to preserve her legacy? If he turns Carter down now, he may never get another chance.

"Yes," he whispers then speaks more firmly. "Yes, Melissa deserves this. Please, write about her in...in the most artistic way you can. Make her," he struggles to find the right words, "make her seem alive again, will you?"

Carter's pasty face is flushed red, his freckles magnified by his tears. "I will do my absolute best, Tom. I will give it my all."

Thomas nods, a sob burning in his throat. This is it. Everything is falling into place, but the end for Melissa is final. How can he ever say goodbye? He looks at Benjamin and Jas, his emotions mirrored in their eyes.

The pain will never end if they continue to fight alone. They must join hands, commiserate together, and share each other's burdens. There is no other way to fully heal.

He reaches over to awkwardly hug his uncle's side. "Ready to go home, Uncle Ben?"

Ben nods, his age showing in the lines around his mouth. "Yes, Tommy, I think that would do us all good."

Officer Holmes sees them out. "If there is anything else, you need just to call. I'll keep in contact as well."

"Thank you, officer. I can't say how much this means to us."

"No problem, Ben." He gives them all a final smile in parting. "You all take care now."

The house is a comfort, its musty odor enveloping Thomas as they walk inside. It may not be perfect, but the memories it holds, the secrets it could tell, those are what is perfect. Sometimes, in searching for perfection, we lose sight of what really matters in this life, and that is love. Thomas turns around to face Benjamin and Jas. He breathes in deeply, releasing his tension in one long breath. "It is good to be home."

30

J as laughs lightly, tears glittering in her grey eyes. "Yes, it really does."

Ben watches them laughing, happiness gleaming in his own eyes. "All right, you two, let's go to bed early, all right?"

Thomas wants to stay up late, to cherish this good mood. But exhaustion overwhelms him, and he makes his way to bed, ignoring the shower. He opens the window above his bed to breathe in the refreshing air, earthy but invigorating. The comforter hides him from the chill, the moonlight casts shadows on the walls.

It feels so peaceful that the last few days could have just been a nightmare. But it is real, and we should never allow ourselves to forget the painful moments of life because that is how we grow. Thomas feels his eyes growing heavy, giving in to the bliss of dreamless sleep.

He awakes to a brisk wind sending a shower of raindrops onto his face. Closing the window, he jumps out of bed, wide awake now. Realizing he cannot ignore the shower forever, he allows the steamy water to envelop him before dressing himself to head to the kitchen. Jas is already there in her chair, a cup of coffee in front of her and another one brewing. She looks up as he enters, her hair wet as well from the shower. "Good morning," she yawns.

He tries to stifle it but yawns as well. "That must be contagious."

She forces a smile, though it comes across looking slightly strained. "Guess so."

Thomas stands there, not sure what to do. For so long, they have been working as a team towards one common goal, but now they are just friends. Friends who know each other's dark secrets, hidden away in painful pasts. As much as he is embarrassed for the shadowy parts he's shown, he does not want to lose Jas.

"Hey, do you think I could maybe have some coffee with you?" He ventures awkwardly.

"That'd be nice, yeah."

They sit there in silence for several minutes. Jas drinks her coffee black like a regular adult, making Thomas feel childish with his creamy sugar mixture tinged with coffee. The walls are covered in cross-stitched pictures, engraved plaques, and framed quotes. He searches for something to start a new conversation, but it is Jas who speaks up first.

"I feel happy here. It's safe, comfortable, and I don't have to be alone." She hesitates as if afraid of what she may say. "But at the same time, I feel guilty. Lisa is dead, and here I am going about life like nothing ever happened.

How dare I allow myself to be happy, to forget her. I should share her pain."

"Why can't you be happy?"

"Don't you feel the same way about Melissa?"

He traces a finger around the edge of his mug, his skin absorbing droplets of coffee. "I did feel that way for a long time," he confesses. "Now that I've thought about it, though, I don't think Melissa would have wanted me to feel guilty. She would have wanted me to find the happiness that she never had. To live life to the fullest and not waste a second of it. They shouldn't die in vain, Jas. I know for sure that Lisa would have wanted you to be happy."

She breaks down sobbing, large sobs that rack her entire body. Thomas watches, stunned, as Jas buries her face in her arms. He touches her back tentatively, making small rhythmic circles in an attempt to be soothing.

"It'll be okay, we just have to keep going."

"What is the next step, though?" Her voice is muffled in her arms.

"That's up to you, Jas. I know what my next step is but...it is going to be tough."

She peeks out at him, her cheeks glistening with tears. "What is it?"

He sighs deeply. "Eventually, I have to call my parents. You know, to tell them what is going on, what we did, and everything."

"The longer you put it off, the more painful it is going to be. Unless you decide not to call, of course."

Thomas knows that she is right. It is only going to become easier to procrastinate if he continues to wait. Besides, what is there to wait for? The clock on the oven says it is eight o'clock. His parents will be awake and starting their day. Reluctantly, he drags himself over to the phone to make the call.

"You are doing it now?" Jas asked incredulously.

"You're right. I can't wait any longer."

Turning his back to Jas, he dials the number, feeling like a trespasser on his past life. The ringing sounds like a death tone, the waiting becoming more agonizing by the millisecond. Finally, a female voice speaks through the receiver.

"Hello, Dendricks."

Thomas's breath catches in his throat. What to say now? He can almost see his mother furrowing her brow, probably thinking it is some telemarketer because she doesn't recognize her brother-in-law's phone number. "Hello?" she says again, more irritably.

"Hey, Mom."

"Thomas?" she gasps. "Oh my gosh, Thomas, where have you been?"

"At Uncle Ben's."

"That man is no good, Thomas. What are you thinking?"

"Oh, so you and dad are anything better?" Thomas retorts. He didn't want to immediately argue, but he is left with no other choice. "Last I recall, you two just made me feel pretty worthless."

"Watch your tone, young man."

"You don't deny it?" Thomas feels the adrenaline coursing through his veins as he bounces lightly on his feet.

"Deny what?" Her exasperated tone echoes in his ear.

"I can't believe it." All of the fight drains out of Thomas in those two words. "After all these days, you still don't know why I left, do you? Well, I'll tell you why. It is because I never have felt wanted anywhere in my entire life because I am just the paranormal freak, right?"

She starts to protest, but he cuts her off. "No, don't you even *try* to say otherwise. I know who I am, but now, I feel like I have a place in this world, and it is not with you and dad. It is with Uncle Ben where I can feel accepted. I can finally be loved for who I am."

He half expects her voice to be choked with tears, but instead, she spits out her next words. "*Accepted?* Thomas Lucas Dendricks, let me tell you right now that you are throwing your life away if you walk away from us now."

"Is there any way to live if you are blinded in a cage?"

"Get some sense into your head, Thomas."

He hears a scuffle on the other end of the phone before hearing his father's voice. "Tom? What on earth have you been doing?" Allen sighs, a sound that grates against Thomas's soul. "Tell us everything right now."

Thomas knows that he is not obligated to tell them anything. After all, they distanced themselves from him first. More than anything, would Melissa want these people to hear the dark, gory details of her fate? Or would she want Thomas to try to do something to open their eyes to the truth?

"All right, I'll tell you." He stares at a scratch on the wall, just something to keep himself grounded. "Melissa Downs was only thirteen years old when she was raped less than a month ago. Yeah, I know you heard about it, but all of that was sugarcoated garbage."

Elise inhales sharply. "Thomas..."

"Don't," he snaps. "Anyhow, her parents made her sound like some slut who just happened to hit on the wrong guy. But that is anything but reality. She was an innocent, sweet, young, beautiful girl who worked hard and cared about school. She was quiet because she felt excluded, but that only made her more pretty. I could...I could relate to her.

"I only wish that I would have had the guts to talk to her, but I never did. But at least I know what really happened to her so that I can tell the *real* story."

"Thomas, girls get raped all the time," his father interjects.

"So...what? That makes it okay?" Thomas is quickly losing his cool, but he doesn't even care anymore. "What about Aunt Helen, huh? Why didn't I ever know I had an aunt who killed herself because she went through rape? But no, it just wasn't important enough because you are all so high and mighty!"

"Don't you *dare* speak to your mother and me like that!"

"Why not!?" Thomas shouts. Jas places a hand on his shoulder to settle him, but he merely shrugs her off without bothering to turn around. "There are countless victims of rape that went to the bridge because of people like *you*! People who never care about anyone but themselves, who lock themselves up in their homes to shut out the negativity of society. Well, I am done living in denial. I am done!"

His father sounds bored, yawning into the receiver. "So...why are you telling us this?"

"I just can't believe this," Thomas whispers incredulously. "You really never will understand."

"Understand what, Thomas?" his mother pleads. "You never make any sense."

"That makes my decision so much easier." Thomas takes a deep breath before releasing it slowly. "I am moving out. I am not wanted by you, so I will stay with Uncle

Ben. No matter what, you'll always want me to change, to conform to your image. Well, I can't. I won't."

There is silence before the other end of the line goes dead. Thomas stares at the phone in his head, willing for something to happen but unsure what it is he even wants to *have* happen. Jas gently reaches over his arm to put the phone back in its charging cradle.

"That was so brave of you, Thomas."

"Yes, it was."

They both jump at the sound of Ben's voice. He is standing by the window, tears streaming down his cheeks. "I hope you will stay as long as you want, Tommy. This... this mess of a house is your home now."

Thomas pushes all formality, all stiffness aside, bounding across the kitchen to wrap his uncle in a hug. He has longed for such a human touch of affection that he had not realized how starved he was for such love.

This is a dream come true, born out of a nightmare. Thomas feels like he has been homeless forever and has finally been found. An aura of comfort washes over him, putting his mind at peace.

Yet how do we define a home? Is it just a building where we sleep, eat, and wash ourselves? No, it is so much more intimate than that. A home is where young couples make their new journeys together, where children grow up building forts in their backyards and igloos in the winter. It is where generations meet around the dinner table at holidays, reminiscing about good times. It is a place of love. For Thomas, he knows this is truly home. Despite its imperfections, Jas is right. This worn down house is full of love. What else could ever compare?

31

Benjamin waves a hand towards Jas. "Come on, join in."

She hesitates, slowly walking towards them with tiny steps. Once she is in reachable distance, Thomas grabs her arm and pulls her into the hug. She squeaks a little, but soon she, too, has melted into the embrace.

"This is home," she whispers into his shirt.

What better image could describe a home? A hug, so warm and connected, full of love and compassion. Thomas feels his eyes welling with tears, choosing to let them fall. For once, they are tears of joy.

Benjamin pulls back slightly. "So, what made you decide to make such a choice?"

"It was Jas, actually." She looks stunned. "No, really, you helped me to realize that I can't put this off any longer. Once I heard their reactions, and how they have not changed, I knew I could never go back."

"Is it wrong to say I'm happy they lost you?"

"No, Uncle Ben, I think that sounds perfectly fine."

He squeezes them all in one last hug before letting go. Jas seems happy, but something is marring it, making it rather bittersweet. Thomas feels his initial joy dimming as he takes in her downcast eyes. "Hey, what's up?"

She looks up, plastering a smile on her face. "Nothing, I'm really happy for you."

"Come off it, what is bothering you?"

Her smile wobbles, a single tear tracing down her cheek. "I...I just wish I had a home like you."

Thomas's mouth drops. "Wait, you're going to stay *homeless*."

"It isn't so bad."

He shakes his head. "It is most definitely bad."

"Thomas is right, Jas. You're staying with us."

"Oh no, I could never infringe..."

"I always wanted a sister," Thomas offers.

She gives him a half smile. "I've heard horror stories about brothers."

"I guess we could at least give it a try."

She sighs overdramatically, throwing up her hands. "Okay, I will stay!"

They all share another hug before breaking down in laughter. All of the pressure of the last few days, weeks, and years just washes away, replaced by relief. For so long they have been walking alone in the darkness, but now, they are found at last.

Alone, they are weak, starved for love. Together, they are strong and filled with hope. Humans are not meant to live in solitude, but rather, we are meant to flourish as a community. Society may try to break that bond, but it shall not prevail.

Looking around, Thomas sees them as a family. Yes, they are a small broken family, but to him it is perfect. Jas is smiling, her grey eyes alight. Benjamin is casually leaning against the table, a small laugh bubbling from his lips.

Together, they will mend their broken pieces and start a new future. A warm glow snakes its way through Thomas's chest. There will always be questions, but for now, he has all the answers he needs. Besides, maybe some things are meant to remain a mystery.

Jas looks over at Thomas, his forehead wrinkled in thought. "How do you like your new family?"

Overwhelming affection for these two causes tears to spring to his eyes. "I love it. I love it so, so much."

"We love you too, Tommy," Ben agrees, clapping a hand fondly on his nephew's shoulder.

The guilt of Helen, Lisa, and Melissa has been shed. There is only so long that we can live in mourning. Then we must step out into the new day and remember them always in our hearts.

Thomas joins in their joyful laughter, knowing that Melissa is at peace. Her memory will live in his heart forever, and for now, that is enough. To ever get out of darkness, one must first find love. He looks at his new family, knowing that the darkness will never reach them here. For in this home, there is love.

END

ABOUT THE AUTHOR

Hannah Klumb is the author of The Suicide Bridge. She is currently studying at Southern New Hampshire University to earn a degree in English in creative writing. However, she decided to follow her heart before waiting to complete her studies and wrote The Suicide Bridge at a Starbucks. She has lived her entire life in central Wisconsin, but would love to see the birthplaces of famous authors around the world.